P9-CFU-524

Journey to the Blue Moon

Journey
to the
Blue
Moon

*In which time is lost
and then found again*

REBECCA RUPP

CANDLEWICK PRESS
CAMBRIDGE, MASSACHUSETTS

First edition 2006

Library of Congress Cataloging-in-Publication Data
Rupp, Rebecca.
Journey to the blue moon / Rebecca Rupp. —1st ed.
p.   cm.
Summary: After a gang of talking rats transports a young boy to the
moon, he embarks on a series of adventures and gains a new
perspective on the concept of time.
ISBN-13: 978-0-7636-2544-3
ISBN-10: 0-7636-2544-2
[1. Time—Fiction. 2. Fantasy.] I. Title.
PZ7.R8886AI 2006
[Fic]—dc22   2005052731

2 4 6 8 10 9 7 5 3 1

Printed in the United States of America

This book was typeset in Garamond.

Candlewick Press
2067 Massachusetts Avenue
Cambridge, Massachusetts 02140

visit us at www.candlewick.com

As always, for Randy, Josh,
Ethan, and Caleb—and for Paulie,
who believed in Alex from the first

Contents

CHAPTER 1

Alex in Trouble

*In which Alex gets a lecture
on the error of his ways*

Alex was in trouble. He knew it even before he reached the living-room door. He could smell it. It was a sort of brimstone-and-burned-rubber smell that made him think of electric chairs.

His parents were sitting next to each other on the living-room couch. Alex's mother had the sad look she always got when Alex had done something really dreadful. His father, who turned red in the face when he was mad, had gone a plummy purple. In one hand he held Alex's latest report card and in the other, an official-looking letter.

"Sit down, Alex," he said in an awful voice.

Alex sat down on the edge of the blue armchair, as far away from the couch as possible.

"We are extremely disappointed in you, Alex," his father said. "Your behavior has been very difficult these past few months. You've missed appointments, forgotten your homework, neglected your chores . . ."

"You've even forgotten to feed the dog," his mother said.

Alex felt a horrible pang of guilt. How could he have forgotten? His dog, Zeke, was his best friend.

"And according to this letter," Alex's father continued—he waved the letter in the air and then dropped it disgustedly on the coffee table as if it were a dead fish—"you have not successfully completed one single school assignment this entire semester. Not one!"

He opened the report card and squinted at it.

"'D,'" he read loudly. "'D. D. D. C. F.'"

"C?" Alex's mother repeated hopefully.

"It's in Phys. Ed.," Alex's father said bitterly. He shook the report card at her. "They give them Cs for breathing."

"We're worried about you, Alex," his mother said. "For months now you've seemed depressed and unhappy. Your teacher says you're not living up to your potential. You spend your time in class staring out the windows. Something must be wrong."

"They don't have these problems at military boarding schools," Alex's father said.

He tossed Alex's report card after the letter.

"Uniforms," he said threateningly. "Shoe polish. Cold showers. Push-ups."

"I'm sure Alex can explain, dear," Alex's mother said hopefully.

Alex was pretty sure that he couldn't.

"I just sort of forgot," he mumbled uncomfortably.

"You just sort of forgot," his father repeated. "You just sort of forgot an entire semester?"

Through the living-room window Alex could see a squirrel running along a branch of a maple tree. He wished he could be a squirrel. Or maybe even a tree. Life could be fun as a tree. He could have fruit or owls or something.

"Alex!" his father said sharply.

Alex sighed.

"Nothing seems important," he said.

"Nothing seems important?" his mother repeated.

Alex shook his head.

"Like all that school stuff," Alex said. "It all seems sort of pointless."

He glanced up at his parents. They were staring at him with their mouths open. Abruptly Alex's father shut his, with a snap.

"That *school stuff,* young man," he said, "is what constitutes a good education. That *school stuff,* as you call it, is the bedrock of civilization. The sum of human knowledge, passed down from generation to generation. I learned it. Your mother learned it. Now it's your turn to learn it."

Alex bit his lip.

"He's having an existential crisis," Alex's mother said to his father. "I think he needs to see a psychiatrist."

"I think he needs a spanking," Alex's father said.

"I keep thinking about time," Alex said. Now that he'd started explaining, he wanted them to understand. "I read somewhere that the average person lives 76.7 years. That's not much time, really. That's seventy-six Christmases and seventy-six birthdays and seventy-six Halloweens. That's 27,995 *days*. Nineteen more if you count leap years. That's all you get. And for half of that you're asleep."

"Your grandmother is eighty-two and in perfect health," Alex's father said.

Alex began to jiggle his foot unhappily. "So everybody starts out with all this time and then it just *vanishes*, minute by minute, and pretty soon it's all gone and there's nothing you can do about it."

Now that he'd started talking, he didn't seem to be able to shut himself up.

"And the more you think about it, the more time seems to go faster and faster. It's like being in a car that's going so fast that you never have a chance to look at all the stuff along the road.

And the road is always disappearing behind you and you can never go back and you'll never have a chance to see it again."

He was beginning to run out of breath. He jiggled his foot faster.

"So it doesn't really matter what we do. Our time just keeps running out and then everything's over. So what's the point of anything?"

"He needs vitamins," said Alex's mother to his father.

"He needs discipline," Alex's father said. "Discipline, structure, and a sense of responsibility. Stop that *jiggling*!"

Alex stopped jiggling his foot.

His father pointed a finger direfully at Alex's chest. "From now on," he said in fearsome tones, "there will be no more of this *time* nonsense. You will come directly home from school each day—*directly,* Alex—and you will go to your room and remain there until dinner doing your homework, which you will then show to me. When you are not occupied with homework, you will be completing—in a timely and efficient manner—your heretofore neglected chores. This slothful behavior will go no further. Do you understand me, Alex?"

"I guess so," Alex said.

"Good," his father said.

Alex's mother nodded.

"You can start by returning your library books, Alex," she said. "They're overdue."

"And don't loiter," his father said. "*That's* what wastes time, Alex. Loitering. Loitering and lollygagging and dragging your feet."

"Be home by six," his mother said.

CHAPTER 2

A Meeting at the Library

*In which Alex has an odd
conversation and receives a token*

Alex was in the library Reading Room.

Nobody ever read in the Reading Room. It was cold and damp, and it was furnished with mournful-looking rubber plants and uncomfortable liver-colored chairs.

Alex was sitting on one of the chairs, beneath a fly-spotted portrait of George Washington. The portrait had been engraved after the Battle of New York, and—if Washington's expression was anything to go by—he had just lost the battle, and was thinking about his pointless life and failed career. Alex knew just how he felt.

He heaved an enormous sigh and fumbled— for the thousandth time—in his right pants pocket, in the empty space that used to contain his pocket watch. The watch still wasn't there. Alex hadn't really expected that it would be. It had been missing for months.

The watch was a family heirloom. It had a silver-plated cover with an engraved picture of an odd little bearded man with two faces, one looking to the right, the other to the left. On the back was a message in an old-fashioned curly script: *Choose time or lose time.* Alex had never understood what that meant. After all, how could you choose time? Time was already chosen for you, wasn't it? And how could you keep from losing it?

The watch had been a present from his grandmother on his tenth birthday. He hadn't told his parents about losing it yet. He just couldn't. A lot of the things he told his parents about turned out to be last straws, and he knew that losing the watch was a perfectly huge last straw.

He sighed again, louder.

As he did, there was a flustered rustling sound from the opposite side of the room.

Alex gave a start of surprise. The room wasn't deserted after all. A head slowly emerged from the depths of an uncomfortable chair as its owner struggled to sit up.

"Oh, dear," the head said fussily. "Oh, dear me. I seem to have dozed off. And what a sight I am, to be sure. 'Tidy habits, orderly mind,' that's what my sister, Selena, always says, 'and what that says about *you*, Lulu,' she says— meaning me, that is—'is as plain as the nose on your face.' Neat as a pin, Selena is, and never a hair out of place, though how she manages I'm sure I don't know. Do you see my purse anywhere around here, dear? And my shopping bag?"

"They're right next to your chair," Alex said. "On the floor."

The speaker wore a rumpled white pullover

and a pair of small silver-rimmed spectacles. Her nose, which was faintly pink, had a tendency to quiver, and she had a tangled shock of cottony white hair. She reminded Alex of the White Rabbit in *Alice in Wonderland*.

"It must be getting late," she said worriedly. She even sounded like the Rabbit. "I don't suppose you happen to have the time?"

"No," Alex said.

The word *time* hit him like a punch in the stomach. All the awfulness of the afternoon crashed in upon him. The look on his face must have given him away, because the Rabbity lady put out a hand in concern.

"Oh, dear," she said unhappily. "I see I've said something very wrong. I often do. I'm always putting my foot in it. My sister, Selena, is forever telling me so. 'Think before you speak,' she says to me, 'and Lulu,' she says—that's what she calls me, dear, Lulu—'Lulu, I never knew a person so absolutely certain to say the wrong thing as you,' and I'm sure she's right. Selena usually is."

"It's not your fault," Alex said.

"Sit down," the Rabbity lady said. She patted the chair beside her. "Sit right down here and tell me all about it, whatever it is. It will make you feel better. 'Share your troubles,' Selena says, 'and halve the load.' Which makes a lot of sense when you think about it. She's very sensible, Selena is. And call me Lulu, dear, do."

Alex sat down and found himself telling Lulu everything. For a talkative person, she was a surprisingly good listener. She pursed her lips as he explained, shook her head sadly when he recounted what his parents had said, nodded sympathetically in all the right places, and gave an excited little bounce in her seat when he described his lost pocket watch with its peculiar saying: *Choose time or lose time.*

"Why, *that's* your problem, dear, don't you see?" she cried brightly. "That's why everything's in such a tizzy. It went with the watch, you see. It happens all the time, dear, you mark my words. Why, we met a painter once who'd lost his perspective along with his paintbrush, and a sorry state he was in, and there was a whole troupe of acrobats who lost their balance when the laundry misplaced their leotards. You'll have to go and fetch it, of course, to set things back to rights, but that's only fair, and a valuable lesson learned. 'If it comes too easily, you won't appreciate it,' Selena says, and 'No gain without pain,' which used to drive me positively wild when I was a child, but she's quite right, you know, dear, quite right."

"I don't understand," Alex said. "What do you mean, go and fetch it? How can I fetch it? Fetch it from *where*?"

"Why, from the Moon, of course, dear," Lulu said, opening her eyes very wide. "That's where all lost things go. To the Moon. You just wait until it turns blue, which should be happening any night now, and then off you go. With a spot of luck, you find what you're after and back before morning, with no one the wiser. 'What they don't know won't hurt them,' that's what Selena used to say. She was a bit of a scamp in her younger days, though you'd never know it to hear her now."

She reached down, picked up the large black purse on the floor next to her chair, opened it, and began to root around inside. Alex glanced nervously toward the door. The Rabbity lady was clearly batty. What if she pulled out a knife or something? He hoped, if push came to shove, that he'd be able to outrun her, but on the other hand, he wasn't certain that he could. She looked pretty spry.

"The Moon turns blue?" he asked. *Keep her talking,* he thought. Surreptitiously he wiggled forward in his seat.

Lulu snapped the purse shut with an air of having found what she was looking for and sat up.

"Well, of course it does, dear. One of our visitors explained it all once. A lovely man, though a bit difficult to understand, to my way of thinking. Still, Selena seemed to follow him well enough, such a head for facts and figures she has, and perfectly comfortable with *interdimensional transport* and *temporal translocation* and all the rest of it. That's what the Blue is, dear; it's when the door opens up in space-time between us and them—or rather, us and you, that is— and when we begin to come into the Blue, that's when we can travel back and forth, see the sights, do a bit of shopping."

"Sure," Alex said. He took a deep breath. "Could you tell me how to *get* to the Moon? I mean, it's a long way away."

"Oh, mercy, there's no need to worry about *that,* dear, none at all," Lulu chirped, sitting up very straight in her chair. "There's ways and ways. Something turns up for everyone, if they're a likely candidate, that is, and you'd be amazed, my dear, *amazed* at what gets pressed into service, though all roads lead to Rome, in a matter of speaking, and it hardly matters once you get there, if you take my meaning."

Alex wasn't sure that he did, but he didn't get a chance to say so.

Lulu leaned forward suddenly and clutched his arm. Alex noticed that her fingertips sparkled slightly.

"Of course, it's not *easy,* dear," she said in a rapid whisper. "There's a lot out looking for time these days, in a manner of speaking, and some of them not at all nice. But you'll be all right if you pass time by and then pass through it. Can you remember that, dear? And you'll have to beware of Urd."

"Urd?" Alex repeated blankly.

But the Rabbity lady had picked up her shopping bag, tucked her purse firmly under one arm, and was hastening toward the door.

"Well, dear, I must be going. It's been a pleasure chatting with you, but it's late, you know, and Selena gets huffy if I'm late. Still, when I explain, she'll be glad to hear that I could be of help. You just wait until it's full blue, mind, not a moment before, and then you've got three days more or less to do your hunting before the way goes shut. A bit like hide-and-seek, but with a prize at the end."

Just as she reached the door, she turned, hurried back to Alex, and pressed something into his hand.

"I was almost forgetting," she said. "You'll need that, dear. Just show it at the gate. I'd forget my head if it weren't screwed on tight— that's what Selena is always telling me. Now I really must dash. Best of luck, dear."

And with that, she was out the door at a run.

Alex stood for a moment, staring at the floor where she had stood. The boards were powdered with glittery bluish dust.

Then slowly he opened his hand. He held a flat plastic token about the size of a fifty-cent piece. It was a dull silvery gray and had little ridges all around the edge, like a checker. On one side, in capital letters, it said: ADMIT ONE.

CHAPTER 3

Rats in the Night

*In which Alex has
unexpected visitors*

The next week was miserable. Alex was made to
follow a schedule posted on the family refrigera-
tor, in which every moment of his day was accounted for in labeled fifteen-minute blocks. He
had to check them off one by one in red pencil.
The check marks seemed to make his parents
happier, but they didn't make Alex feel any better. He had a continual whooshing feeling, as if
time were rushing past his ears and then disap-

pearing, like water gurgling down a drain. Sometimes this made him feel panicky and desperate, but more often he just felt hopeless and tired. Zeke followed him around worriedly, bringing him sticks and damp dog biscuits.

Then one night he had a dream.

In the dream he was a drummer in a marching band, but he didn't have any drumsticks and he couldn't keep up with the other marchers. His feet felt as if they were slogging through molasses. Then one of the marchers in front of him turned around, and suddenly it was the Rabbity lady from the library, wearing a band uniform cap with a lot of gold braid on the brim. "Remember, dear, it has to be blue," she said, and then the cymbal player, who looked a little bit like George Washington, clashed his cymbals together right in Alex's ear.

He woke up, heart pounding, to the sound of cymbals outside his window. No, not cymbals. It sounded as if somebody were pounding on the garbage can lids. Alex sat up and peered outside. He could just see white shapes, moving purposefully around behind the garage. There seemed to be four or five of them. *Raccoons?* Alex thought. He pressed his nose to the window. *Burglars?* If so, they seemed to be very *short* burglars. And what were they doing with the garbage cans?

The bedsprings moaned protestingly as Zeke clambered awkwardly onto the bed to sit beside him. Zeke wasn't ordinarily allowed on the bed, but Alex made exceptions for things like nightmares and thunderstorms and the time there was a scritchy little noise in the ceiling that might just possibly have been a vampire bat. Zeke poked his nose into Alex's ribs and gave an inquiring whine.

"Hush," Alex told him. "I want to see what's out there."

There was a sudden explosion of activity behind the garage and a chorus of outraged squeaks. The—small burglars?—appeared to be scuffling. Then one of the shapes shot backward out of the shadows into the moonlight. It staggered, tottered, and sat down heavily in the grass with its legs splayed out in front of it. It seemed to have been pushed.

Alex gaped in astonishment.

It was a rat.

The creature was about three feet tall, with a long silvery tail and short white fur that had a luminous shimmer, as if it had been dusted all over with sugar. It was wearing a tool belt and a pair of cracked aviator goggles, which were fastened behind its ears with a knotted piece of string. As Alex watched, it scrambled to its feet and began to jump up and down, furiously shaking its fists.

Zeke gave a startled yip and put a paw over his head. Alex slid hastily off the bed, threw on his jeans, stuffed his feet into his sneakers, and tugged a sweater over his pajama shirt.

"Come on," he said to Zeke. "Let's see what's going on."

They padded rapidly down the back stairs and silently let themselves out the kitchen door. The backyard was flooded with moonlight. It was so bright that the trees and bushes cast dark shadows on the glimmering ground. Alex edged forward cautiously, his fingers clutching Zeke's collar.

The rats were still there. He could see their

shadows moving confusedly back and forth. There was another crash from behind the garage, an angry squeak, and the sound of voices squabbling.

"We need the round one, I tell you! And that one over there, with all the little screws in it. Not that one, knucklehead! The one next to it."

"I've got it! I've got it! *Ouch!* Give that back!"

"Stop *pulling!*"

"Move *over,* Perline! You're standing on my—"

"I saw it first!"

"Ouch!"

Zeke began to growl low in his throat. The squabbling instantly ceased. There was a moment of frozen silence. Then a high nervous voice asked shakily, "Is anybody there?"

Zeke pulled insistently on his collar and growled louder.

There was a hasty mutter of voices, then the nervous voice took on a pompous artificial tone. "No need to be alarmed, sir or madam," it said rapidly. "Just a matter of routine. We're— meter readers. That's all we are. Meter readers."

"That's right," another voice put in helpfully. "Meter readers."

"Here to read your meter."

With a ferocious tug, Zeke broke loose from Alex's grasp and galloped toward the voices, barking. There was a chorus of shrieks, and rats scattered across the lawn.

"Zeke!" Alex shouted. *"Stop that!"*

He dashed forward and flung himself on the dog. Zeke struggled frantically, with pleading yelps that signaled excitement, frustration, and a sacrificial willingness to protect Alex from certain death by eating the intruders. Alex got a firm grip on his collar and hung on.

"It's all right," he called. "You can come out. I've got him."

The rats pattered out slowly, sticking very close together and muttering to each other in squeaky undertones. They formed a ragged line in front of Alex and Zeke. Their silvery whiskers and beady little silver eyes glinted metallically in the moonlight.

Each rat clutched an armful of scraps gleaned from the trash. They had the wheels from the old push lawn mower, the broken pieces from Alex's discarded Erector set, empty paint cans, and a lot of bent pipes and rusty springs and twisted rolls of torn chicken wire. The smallest rat—the one with the aviator goggles—was hugging a dented hubcap.

"Who *are* you?" Alex asked incredulously. "And what are you doing with all that junk?"

There was a flurry of pushing, poking, and prodding.

"You tell him, Scrubber."

"Go on, Scrubber. Speak up."

The biggest rat sighed.

"Meter readers," he said bitterly. " 'It's a stupid story,' I said. 'They'll never believe it,' I said. 'So put it to a vote,' you said. So we did. And see what happens." He pointed accusingly at Alex and Zeke. "Human beings is what happens. And *dogs.*"

"Who *are* you?" Alex asked again.

The biggest rat puffed out his chest and raised his voice. "We're Moon Rats," he said impressively. "From the—you know—Moon."

He gestured upward with his nose toward the Moon, which inconveniently chose that moment to hide behind a cloud.

"But we're just here for a quick visit, see? Here and back again and no harm done. Hardly worth mentioning that you've seen us, is it, if She—if anyone should ask? By tomorrow morning it will be as if none of this ever happened. Leave nothing but footprints, we do, and take any litter with us."

A plumpish Moon Rat in a carpenter's apron who had dropped a bubblegum wrapper in the grass hastily covered it with his foot.

"We clean up, like."

"Remove unwanted items."

"It's a service, see?"

"I won't tell anybody," Alex said. "Do you have names?"

"That's Scrubber," one of the shorter rats said, pointing at the speaker. It was a female rat, Alex guessed. She was wearing a cracked pink bicycle helmet secured under her chin with a rubber band. She moved closer to Alex and lowered her voice. "Likes to have his own way, he does, but we watches him. And I'm Perline, and this here is Elveeta."

Elveeta was wearing a very small cardigan sweater with several buttons missing and a pair of mismatched mittens. She waved one at Alex.

"That one over there is Opie"—she pointed at the plump rat still standing sheepishly on the bubblegum wrapper—"and the little runt on the end is Tetley."

Everybody turned to look at Tetley, who turned pinkish and dropped his hubcap.

"I'm Alex," Alex said. "And this is my dog, Zeke."

A thought struck him.

"How did you all get here?" he asked. "All the way from the Moon?"

The rats, moving as one, turned and pointed.

"In that," Perline said proudly.

Alex looked in the direction of the pointing paws.

Under the oak tree in the far corner of the backyard was a spaceship. Or at least, if you used enough imagination, it looked sort of like a spaceship. If you didn't use imagination, it looked like a heap of scrap metal.

It was cobbled together from a wild array of discarded bits and pieces. There were struts and flaps and coils and knobs and a row of useless-looking gratings that appeared to have come from an old-fashioned iron kitchen stove. The body of the ship, however, seemed surprisingly solid. Beneath the gratings, which were held in place by a miscellaneous jumble of bolts, screws, rivets, cotter pins, and—in one place— a bent fork, Alex could just make out the letters *ASA*.

"We found it, we did," Perline said smugly.

"Then we improved on it, like."

"Took a whole month."

"Would have been less if you hadn't knocked the tail fins off."

"Didn't. It was Opie."

"Was not."

"Was too."

"It's very nice," Alex interrupted hastily. "I've never seen anything like it." That was certainly true, he reflected.

"Time we was off," Scrubber said briskly. "Before anything else happens, that is."

"Well, it was nice meeting you," Alex said awkwardly.

"Same here," Scrubber said. He held out a limp paw, and Alex shook it. "Until we meet again and all that."

"He could come along with us," Perline said, stepping in front of them. "For a visit, see? Because he was so nice and all."

"Plenty of room."

"He can have my seat. Because I'll be navigating, see?"

"No, you won't. It's not your turn."

"Is too."

"Is not."

Zeke pawed Alex's ankle and gave a warning yelp, signaling his opinion of reckless journeys taken with oversized bickering rats in rattletrap spaceships. "Don't be stupid," that yelp said. Alex couldn't help but see his point. But a part of him was tempted.

What could it hurt? he thought. *It can't be*

that dangerous. After all, the rats got here all right.

The rats were pushing each other, squeaking, and pointing excitedly overhead.

"There it is!"

"I saw it first!"

"No, me!"

"*You* wouldn't have seen it if it bit your backside!"

"Would too!"

"Would not!"

Alex followed their pointing paws. A full moon had moved majestically out from behind its covering blanket of cloud. He could barely believe his eyes.

It was blue.

CHAPTER 4

To the Blue Moon

*In which Alex embarks
on a journey*

The spaceship sounded as if it were falling apart. It shuddered and shrieked, rattled, screeched, and clanked. Inside, it was stuffy and overcrowded. Somebody's paw always seemed to be in Alex's stomach, and somebody's tail kept smacking him in the face.

The cabin was lit with frayed strings of colored Christmas-tree lights that popped and fizzed and kept flickering off and on. The flickers made the rats look jerky, like projected scenes from an old movie. First there was a flashing shot of red rats pouring red fluid from gallon jugs into a fuel tank; then suddenly there were green rats squabbling over green dials on a control panel, and then blue rats clambering on top of each other to pile into a blue row of children's lawn chairs.

The lawn chairs were bolted crookedly to the floor and were equipped with seat belts made from pieces of old clothesline. The belts didn't look very effective, but Alex was wearing his anyway. He was scrunched into the lawn chair at the far end of the row, with Zeke wedged as far as possible underneath the seat. Since the chair was small and Zeke was large, this meant that a lot of Zeke stuck out into the center of the ship, to be sat upon, climbed upon, and fallen over by rats.

The chair was directly in front of a glass porthole, which seemed to be made from a discarded washing-machine door. For a long time now there had been nothing outside that porthole but black night, dotted with distant stars. In the chair beside Alex, Tetley was sound asleep, with his legs stuck straight out in front of him and his hubcap over his face. He was snoring, and whenever he snored, his hubcap quivered. Eventually Alex must have dozed off himself, because he was jerked awake by the sound of a loud squawk from Perline.

"Fins *down,* see? And turn the arrow to the left!"

"No, not that way, you great lumphead!"

"Give me that!"

"It's stuck!"

"Ouch!"

Scrubber was banging on something with a rusty wrench.

Alex sat up, rubbing his eyes. The porthole was filled with a broad expanse of deep blue, and Alex had a fleeting glimpse of mountains, crags, and craters. The spaceship gave a violent hiccup, turned sickeningly upside down, and began to pick up speed.

Alex poked Tetley in the ribs.

"Wake up!" he said. "I think we're crashing!"

Tetley peered out blearily from behind his hubcap, shaking his head.

"Landing, us is," he said.

Perline and Elveeta were shrieking cheerily at the control panel.

"Coming in for a landing!"

"One—two—three—"

"No, not that way, you idiot! Like this, see? Ten—nine—eight—"

"Four!"

"Seven!"

The spaceship bounced twice, made an embarrassing raspberry sound, thudded heavily, and skidded wildly to a stop. Perline and Elveeta fell down in a heap (simultaneously shouting "Five!" and "Six!") and Scrubber staggered backward, tripping over Zeke and dropping his wrench. A cacophony of crashes sounded from the back.

"We're here, see?" Opie said after a moment.

"Everybody out now."

"Can't. The door's stuck."

"Well, kick it."

"*Ouch!* Watch your feet, you great—"

The door burst abruptly open, and rats tumbled out, squealing. Alex and a reluctant Zeke followed.

At first all he saw was blue.

The Moon was wrapped in a shifting blue mist that sometimes thinned and lifted in places to reveal shadowy shapes in the distance, then closed in again in an impenetrable aquamarine fog. The ground beneath his feet was coated with a soft sparkly bluish dust. Stepping in it felt like wading through talcum powder or very fine beach sand. Alex could feel it sifting through his sneakers.

The dust spurted up in powdery little clouds as the rats unloaded their cargo, flinging pipes and paint cans out of the spaceship to accumulate in disorderly heaps on the ground. Zeke yipped and dodged as a broken bedspring grazed his head, hit the dust, recoiled, and bounced off into the fog.

"What happens now?" Alex asked uncertainly. He was beginning to regret his hasty decision to accompany the rats.

The rats all pointed at once.

"You have to go that way, see?"

"To report in, like."

"Down the path, see?"

The mist drifted sluggishly aside, and Alex saw a winding path dwindling into the distance, lined on both sides by tiny twinkling white lights.

"Watch out for the Time Eaters, see?"

"Nasty scary blokes, they is."

"Got my Uncle Elmo, one did."

"Horrible faces they have, like this"—Opie pulled his cheeks in and managed to look hideously mummified. Tetley gave a squeak of distress.

"Suck the life right out of you, they do. Like you was lemonade in a bottle."

"Nothing but a husk left after."

"Shouldn't have to go traveling about alone, he shouldn't. Being new here and all."

The rats put their heads together and consulted rapidly in agitated whispers.

"Tetley can go with him," Scrubber said. "Might as well. He can't carry much anyway."

"Too right."

"Little squirt, he is."

"And no need to mention this to You-Know-Who."

"About the ship and all."

"You two run along," Perline said brightly. "You can catch up with us later."

"Where are we going?" Alex asked, bewildered.

But the rats, laden with their bits and pieces of junk, were already pattering rapidly away, chattering among themselves. Alex looked down at Tetley, standing glumly by the gaping spaceship door, silver tail drooping, still clutching his hubcap.

"Us might as well go," Tetley said in a dismal voice.

They set off along the twinkling little path, Tetley plodding ahead, muttering miserably to himself.

"'Just a runt,' they says. 'Can't carry much,' they says. Laugh at me, they do. 'All in good fun, Tetley,' they says. 'Have a sense of humor, Tetley,' they says. 'Look on the bright side,' they says. But when I ask where all this bright side is, they can't tell me, see? Because there isn't any bright side, see?"

Alex began to feel sorry for Tetley.

"We're here, we is," Tetley said.

CHAPTER 5

The House of Records

*In which Alex meets the Head Clerk
and finds a list of lost things*

They were standing in front of an iron gate. Beyond the gate, through shifting curtains of blue mist, Alex could just make out lumpy shapes of shrubbery.

He squinted, trying to see farther. Then the mist thinned and lifted, rising higher and higher, and Alex saw, towering awesomely above him, the immense stone façade of what looked like a Gothic cathedral.

Enormous stone towers and spires soared to unimaginable heights. Looking up at them made Alex feel dizzy. There were huge arched doorways, a mammoth rose window set with leaded glass, and eaves and ledges ornamented with the carved stone figures of strange animals with wings, beaks, clawed paws, and long serpentine tails.

Alex gaped upward in amazement, craning his neck.

"What *is* this place?" he asked in an awed voice.

"This is the House of Records, this is," Tetley said, sounding like a wet rag. "Everything that comes to the Moon, they write it down on a list in there. They'll write you down, too, see? Everything's in there, it is, written down on a list. And then if you leave, they'll check you off again."

Alex wasn't sure he liked the sound of that. Especially the *if*.

"First we rings the bell, see?" Tetley said.

He stood on tiptoe, stretched one paw over his head, and pressed a large silver button set in one side of the gate. For a long moment nothing happened.

Then there was a whirring sound of wings and a large black bat landed above them on top of the gate. At least a sort of a bat. It had membranous bat wings, a narrow furry face with a curved beak, round silvery eyes, and clawed paws. It blinked twice, folded its wings flat across its back with a sound like a collapsing umbrella, and spoke rapidly as if reciting a prepared speech.

"Welcome to the House of Records," it said. "Home of the universe's greatest known annotated compendium of the mislaid, misplaced, abstracted, translocated, dispersed, dissipated, decamped, squandered, expended, forfeited, or lost. Petitioners welcome. Tours by appointment. Identification card or admission ticket, please."

Tetley fumbled in the pouches of his tool belt and produced a tattered driver's license. The word CANCELED was stamped across it in big red letters and someone had drawn whiskers and a pair of buggy-looking dark glasses on the face in the license photograph with a black felt-tip marker.

The bat seized it in a clawed paw.

"Identification card acceptable," it said. It handed the license back and looked expectantly at Alex.

Alex rummaged in his pocket and tentatively produced the Rabbity lady's plastic token.

"That's it," Tetley said. "ADMIT ONE, see?"

"What about Zeke?" Alex said.

"Canines, felines, and all household pets admissible with owner," the bat babbled. "Unless lost, in which case report to rear of building. Zoo, circus, and menagerie animals, ditto. Special cases, see Pamphlet C."

It snatched Alex's token, tucked it under one arm, snapped its wings open, and rose into the air.

"Please proceed to the Reception Hall," it said, and whirred away.

Alex took a grip on Zeke's collar.

Before them, with a painful screechy sound, the iron gate swung open.

* * *

They stood just inside the massive doorway of the House of Records, looking in and up. A vast dusty flagstone floor stretched away in front of them as far as their eyes could see, and on either side, shelf upon shelf of leather-bound books rose up in tiers, climbing ever upward until they vanished in gloom up toward the distant ceiling. Odd silvery cobwebs hung in festoons from shadowy corners.

The immense room was empty. There was not so much as a flicker of movement. The place gave Alex a creepy feeling at the back of his neck.

"Is anybody here?" he asked Tetley.

His voice echoed in vast dimness. *Here . . . here . . . here . . .*

"I hopes not," whispered Tetley hopefully.

"Welcome," a hoarse voice said behind them. The speaker sounded as if his throat were full of dust.

Zeke yipped, Tetley squeaked, and Alex spun around.

Nobody was there.

"Up here," the voice said.

Alex looked up. Perched high on a ladder to the right of the doorway was a tall spindly man balancing a clipboard on his knees. He was wearing leather sandals, a gray wool robe tied with a sash around the middle, and a pair of thick spectacles. He had very long arms and legs. As he unfolded himself to climb down, Alex was reminded of gangly things like giraffes and camels and telescope tripods.

"I am the Head Clerk," the man said, rapidly descending. "Directly reporting to the Goddess of the Moon."

Tetley dodged behind Alex and began to quiver.

"Who is *not*," the Clerk continued, "in residence at this time."

"Stop it, Tetley," Alex whispered.

The Clerk's sandals made little slapping noises on the flagstones as he walked toward them. He brandished his clipboard in the air.

"Any questions you may have should be referred to me. First, of course, I need to know your names, ages, and the nature of the item you have lost. Is it animal, vegetable, or mineral?

Is it an experience, perhaps, a memory misplaced from the days of your youth? Is it a work unfinished, a promise unfulfilled, an appointment broken, or road not traveled? Or"—he suddenly seemed to focus on Alex—"a misplaced ball, a mislaid mitten, or a carried-off kite? Have you wasted your fortune, spilled your milk, or lost your marbles?"

"Not exactly," Alex said. "I . . ."

But the Clerk had whirled away, gesturing extravagantly with his long arms.

"It's all here," he said. "Everything lost, misplaced, mislaid, abandoned, neglected, unfinished, or foolishly thrown away. Every dropped pin, dropped stitch, and dropped name; every lost letter, lost love, lost hope, lost battle, lost reputation, and all the ships lost at sea. All the things that slide through holes in pockets are here; and everything that slips down cracks or falls off windowsills or blows away in the wind. All here, every last scrap of it, cataloged, recorded, and waiting for collection, though"— his face fell—"hardly anybody ever comes to collect."

"It's all *here*?" Alex said. He looked blankly around the hall. "All the ships and stuff?"

The Clerk shook his head impatiently. "In a manner of speaking, of course," he said. "The record of its *arrival* is here; its precise lunar location"—he waved his fingers vaguely in opposite directions—"is not my province."

He pulled a silver ballpoint pen from a pocket in his robe.

"Last name first, please," he said. "And state your age."

"Bailey, Alexander," Alex said. "I'm eleven."

He paused while the Clerk scribbled on the clipboard.

"And I'm looking for a lost watch. A pocket watch. About this big, on a chain. It has a motto on it. *Choose time or lose time.*"

"Ah," the Clerk said, making a note with his pen. He flexed his elbows and tilted his head sharply to one side, which made him look like an oversized stork.

"It's simply a matter of attending to detail, you know," he said severely. "No one ever loses time who pays attention to detail. You should make lists. A well-thought-out list, prioritized, checked off as each item is completed—that's the way to manage time. Never a lost moment when one has a list."

He sounded, Alex thought, a lot like his parents.

"Is my watch here?" he asked impatiently.

"Oh, it's *here*," the Clerk said. "That is, not right *here*, per se, but *around*."

He bounded across the hall, scampered up a ladder propped against the left-hand wall, and ran his finger quickly along a dusty row of books. He chose one volume, pulled it out, opened it, and began flipping through the pages.

"Here it is," he said. "'Watch: one, pocket. Silver; engraved case and motto; hand-wound; crystal face with brass minute and second hands; six-inch chain.'"

He fell silent for a moment, reading.

"Is that all you're looking for?" he asked. "There are a lot of other items listed."

"Like what?" Alex said.

The Clerk began to read very rapidly.

"'One glove: navy blue, left hand, thumb slightly raveled. Fifty-five cents in change in envelope labeled *Milk Money*. Eleven pens: five black, four blue, two red. One metal lunch box with purple animal motif, containing thermos, apple, chocolate chip cookie, and tuna fish sandwich. One sweater: green, size M. Fourteen small plastic blocks: mixed sizes and colors. Seven puzzle pieces: assorted. Balloon: one, helium, string broken, orange with Happy Birthday message. One workbook: incomplete, arithmetic. One sneaker: blue, right foot. One model rocket: dented, parachute undeployed. Three checkers: two black, one red. One house key: brass. One hamster: brown, answers to name of Rodney.'"

"My hamster?" Alex said. "My hamster is *here*?"

"Not right *here*," the Clerk said, peering irritably at Alex over the tops of his spectacles. "It's around somewhere, though." He glanced back down at the book. "Shall I go on?"

"I don't think so," Alex said. "Thank you anyway."

The Clerk closed the book briskly and tucked it fussily back in place on the shelf.

"So how do I get my watch back?" Alex asked. "I don't understand. If everything's all written down in there, how come you don't know where things *are?*"

A peevish expression came over the Clerk's face.

"I explained that," he said crossly. "It's not my province. That's your problem. Please follow me."

He set out at a trot down the long hall, with Alex, Tetley, and Zeke trotting behind him, struggling to keep up. The struggle was hardest for Tetley, who had the shortest legs.

On either side of them loomed row upon row of towering bookshelves. At intervals, high above them, distant narrow windows let in thin trickles of faint bluish light. More of the odd-looking bats flapped and chattered in the upper rafters.

They passed shelves of black-bound books trimmed with gold stripes, blue-bound books trimmed with silver stars, plain brown books that looked as if something had been chewing on them, and cream-colored books with indecipherable titles stamped in green. There was an enormous cabinet filled with hundreds of tiny drawers and then a row of massive padlocked cupboards and then more bookshelves again.

At last the Clerk turned a corner and ducked down a corridor lined with limp blue velvet curtains. At the end of the corridor he stopped before a wooden door with a silver doorknob in the center shaped like a crescent moon. Alex, Zeke, and—after a frantic pattering interval—Tetley skidded awkwardly to a halt behind him.

"You'll need this," the Clerk said. "It explains everything."

He fumbled in a pocket of his robe and produced a printed card. He handed it to Alex.

The Rules, Alex read to himself.

1. *Searchers may reclaim their lost items only while the Moon is blue.*
2. *Searchers may leave the Moon only after their lost item has been successfully reclaimed.*
3. *Searchers who fail to reclaim their*

*lost item must remain on the
Moon until the next Blue.*

4. *After reclaiming their lost item,
searchers must report back to the
House of Records for immediate
transport to their time and place
of origin.*

"Wait a minute," Alex said worriedly. "You mean if I don't find my watch, I have to *stay* here?" Had Lulu told him that? Zeke gave a horrified yelp.

"How often does the Moon turn blue?"

"Once every century or two," the Clerk said. He slid back a bolt and pulled the door open. "This way now. Move along, please. No time to waste."

"And watch out for the Miasma," he added.

Alex, Zeke, and Tetley stepped across the threshold. Instantly the Clerk slammed the door behind them, nearly catching the tip of Tetley's tail.

Through the wooden panels, they heard the sharp click of the lock.

Alex turned and pounded furiously on the locked door.

"Hey! Come back!" he shouted.

What kind of a mess was he in now? He might never get home again. He and Zeke could be trapped here on the Moon forever.

"What am I supposed to do now? At least tell me where I'm supposed to *go*!"

The only reply was the muffled sound of the Clerk's retreating footsteps.

CHAPTER 6

Companions

*In which Alex and Tetley
make some new friends*

As they moved away from the Clerk's locked door, Alex, Zeke, and Tetley found themselves in a marble courtyard lit with a cold bluish light. The marble slabs of the paved floor underfoot gleamed and glittered with blue highlights and strange shadows. It looked like a skating rink covered with funny-colored ice.

The courtyard was surrounded by a tall iron fence with an even taller iron gate, and on either side of the gate were two marble benches with carved lions' paws for feet. As they watched, the gate, with a rusty shriek, flung itself abruptly open and hung there on its hinges, quivering.

"We goes out that way, see?" Tetley said helpfully.

"I see," Alex said.

Outside the gate, a blue fog began to rise. First it coiled up damply around Alex's ankles, then it rose to his knees. At the same time, swaths and curtains of mist closed in around them from all sides, drifting toward them over the dusty ground like oozing crowds of outsized blue ghosts. Soon Alex couldn't see his hand in front of his face.

"Stick together, everybody," he said. "Or we'll lose each other."

"I is lost now," Tetley said in a nervous voice. It sounded like it was coming from Alex's right.

"Stay where you are and I'll find you," Alex said. "Keep talking, Tetley. Say something."

"There is other people here," Tetley said, sounding more nervous than ever. "I bumped into they." Now his voice seemed to be coming from the left.

"Stay *still*, Tetley," Alex said.

Was this the Miasma? He might as well have been wearing a blindfold. Nothing was visible through the blue murk. He had lost all sense of time and direction. *A hundred people could be lost in here,* he thought, *and we could wander around forever and never find each other.* He began to wish that he'd never laid eyes on the lady in the library or the Moon Rats. He could have choked the Head Clerk. Then from somewhere far in front of him, Zeke began to bark.

"*Stay*, Zeke!" Alex shouted. "Wait for us!"

A receding thump of paws indicated that Zeke was not doing as he had been told. Alex started to run blindly forward through the fog and promptly collided with Tetley, who was running blindly backward. Tetley shrieked.

"It's just me," Alex said irritably. "Come on, Tetley, give me your paw. We have to find Zeke and get out of this stuff. Which way do you think we should go?"

"Home," Tetley said unhelpfully.

"I think Zeke is somewhere over that way," Alex said. "*Zeke!* Here, boy!"

Far in the distance they could hear barking. They groped their way slowly toward it. The barking grew louder. And the fog, Alex realized with a surge of hope, was getting lighter. It was thinning, fading from indigo to sky blue to a sort of misty azure. The barking grew louder still. Then suddenly, almost between one step and the next, they were in the clear.

Before them was a strange and desolate landscape of dust, craters, and tumbled rocks. The fog hung in the air behind them like a thick blue curtain, billowing slightly, as if something were bumping against it from the inside. Peering into it, Alex thought for a moment that he could see shadowy shapes groping.

"Over here!" he shouted. "This way!"

But the shapes retreated hurriedly and then vanished, swallowed into the depths of the fog.

"There is a people," Tetley said nervously.

Alex turned and stared.

Several yards away from them, holding tightly to Zeke's collar, stood a youngish woman. She was dressed in button boots with pointy toes, a long pink dress with a bustle, and a straw hat trimmed with painted cherries. Under one arm, she carried a rolled-up pink parasol. She looked alert, sensible, and pleasant-tempered, though she wasn't pretty exactly, since her nose was a bit too long and thin and her eyes set a bit too close together. Zeke was happily wagging his tail.

"Is this your dog?" she asked.

Zeke rolled over on his back and put his paws in the air.

Alex nodded. "His name is Zeke," he said.

The pink woman scratched Zeke's belly with her parasol. Zeke wriggled ecstatically.

"Well, I'm sure he saved my life," she said. "I've been wandering in that fog for simply ages."

Zeke gave a satisfied yip.

"I'm Edith Mumsley," the pink woman continued. "*Miss* Edith Mumsley of Picketsville, Ohio. A pleasure to meet you, I'm sure."

Alex introduced himself and, with some difficulty, introduced Tetley, who had gone shy and hidden under his hubcap.

"Are there other people in there?" he asked, pointing back at the foggy curtain.

"Dozens," Miss Mumsley said. "Maybe hundreds. Some have stopped trying to escape and have settled down in there, poor things. Even I was finding it hard not to become discouraged. If it hadn't been for your fine dog here . . ."

"There is another people," said Tetley faintly.

He pointed and then retreated behind Alex, putting his hubcap over his head.

"Oh dear," Miss Mumsley said. "He doesn't look quite well."

Some little distance away, leaning against a rock with his back toward them, was a slumped and dejected-looking figure. As they approached, he turned slowly, pulled his shabby brown velvet robe about him, and made an awkward bow. He had shaggy shoulder-length brown hair under a round velvet cap and sad brown eyes that occasionally drifted into an unfocused faraway look, as if he were studying something unimaginably distant that nobody else could see.

"Your servant, sirs and madam," he said. His voice at first was hoarse and croaky as if he hadn't spoken in a long time. "My name is Simon Nash. A scholar by trade, skilled in the art of alchemy. An indifferent swordsman perhaps, but judged to have some small talent upon the flute. I have been trapped for what seems an eternity in yon misty Miasma, only to have been at last released when I followed the barking of . . ."

"Zeke," Miss Mumsley said. "He belongs to young Alex, here. And this is Tetley—come out from under that hubcap, Tetley. Mr. Nash seems perfectly harmless. And I am Miss Edith Mumsley of Picketsville, Ohio."

A silence fell as they all took stock of each other. Simon, after a moment, drifted into a reverie and began to mumble softly to himself. His eyes went slightly crossed.

"And what did you lose, Alex?" Miss Mumsley finally asked. "You must have lost something. As I understand it, it's the only reason for all of us to be here."

"It's sort of complicated," Alex said. He explained about his missing pocket watch with its confusing message and about his troubles at home. "The lady at the library said that to make things right, I'd have to go to the Blue Moon and find my watch. But it looks like it's going to be harder than I thought. What about you? What did *you* lose?"

"My heart," Miss Mumsley replied promptly.

Then she chuckled at the sight of Alex's startled face.

"I know," she said. "You wouldn't think it to look at me, that I'd go and do a foolish thing like that, but I did, and now there's no help for it but to try and get it back again. I fell in love with a prospector named Jeremiah Stone, who came through Picketsville in 1896 on his way west.

"He was the handsomest man I ever saw, with coal-black hair and eyes as blue as a bluebird wing, and I just fell head over heels the first minute I saw him. He could charm the shoes off a snake, that man could, and me too silly to see it. We'd be married, he said, as soon as he came back rich, and off he went with my savings in his pocket and my granny's gold locket as a luck piece around his neck.

"But first it was gold in Alaska, and next silver in Nevada, and finally diamonds in South Africa, and with one thing and another, he never did come back. At first my heart just broke in two, and then it was gone, lost— *phtt!*—just like that. To tell the truth, there was a time when I thought I'd never want the thing back, troublesome as it's been, but now that I've had a chance to think a bit, I've reconsidered."

"The blackguard," Simon said, coming out of his trance, pulling himself upright, and puffing out his chest. "If ever the villain reappears, my lady, I am at your service."

"Thank you, Mr. Nash," Miss Mumsley said. "But I can quite take care of myself. In any case, I doubt that he'll be back again. The last I heard it was opals in Australia."

"And what about you?" said Alex to Simon.

Simon deflated and looked sheepish.

"I think, young sir," he mumbled unhappily, "that I have lost my way."

"Well, my goodness, Mr. Nash, why didn't you ask directions?" Miss Mumsley exclaimed. "Why, the next person up the street might have solved *your* problem in two shakes of a lamb's tail. Turn left on Elm Street, they might have told you, and saved you all the trouble of traveling to the Moon."

Simon turned a mortified pink.

"It's not that sort of way," he said defensively. "It is a far more tangled way than that, my lady, and not the sort to be unraveled by any simple passerby with a pointing finger."

"Well, what kind of way is it?" Alex said.

Simon cleared his throat and folded his arms across his chest.

"I come from Oxford," he said, "in the Year of Our Lord 1578, the twentieth year of the reign of our good queen Elizabeth, and a fine queen she is, a lady as like her father as two peas in a pod, holding the Spaniards off our shores, soothing the great lords' quarrels, and keeping all England at peace.

"I am not a university student, you understand, but an independent scholar, striving to solve the great puzzles of mathematics, and hoping perhaps to find a way to transmute the earthy element of lead into pure gold. I might have done it, too, using a preparation invented by myself of sulfur, Cyprian copper, hot ash, bismuth, and antimony powder, but one day I fell to musing"—he paused and turned to Alex—"Are you familiar with the mathematics, lad?"

"Sort of," Alex said. "I guess."

"I was calculating the number pi," Simon said impressively, "used to determine the circumference of a circle."

He drew a large circle with his finger in the air, at which Tetley, senselessly, began to giggle.

"But once you begin to calculate pi," Simon said—a despairing note crept into his voice—"it simply goes on and on, number after number, without ever reaching a solution. 3.1415926535897 . . . It never ends. It just goes on and on and on and on and . . ."

"Please, Mr. Nash," Miss Mumsley said.

"Soon I could think of nothing else," Simon said. "My work faltered and came to a halt. How can a number do this, I wondered, all of its own accord? How can a number *never end*?

"And pi isn't alone. The more I studied, the more numbers I found that are just exactly like it.

Repeating fractions. Recalcitrant square roots. Even simple counting does it. Numbers following one after another, number after number, forever. They go on and on and on and on and on . . ."

"Simon," Alex said.

"And on and on and on and on and on and . . ." Tetley said in a singsongy kind of voice, beating time on his hubcap.

Alex stepped warningly on his tail and Tetley stopped with a squeak.

"That's *all*?" asked Miss Mumsley. "*That's* how you lost your way? Over a silly arithmetic problem?"

"*A silly* . . ." Simon began.

He stopped and looked meaningfully at Alex.

"The feminine mind, as everyone knows, is not fitted for intellectual pursuits," he said. "It's no fault of yours," he said kindly to Miss Mumsley. "If you were a man—and indeed a great loss that would be, for one so fair—you would appreciate the earthshaking scope of the problem."

"I think the feminine mind is different now," Alex said. "Since 1578."

"I should say so!" Miss Mumsley said, stepping forward and poking Simon in the chest with her parasol. "Not fitted, indeed! Why, before this century is out, we'll see women get the vote, you mark my words! Women will take their place in all professions and all walks of life. We may even see a woman president one day!"

She raised her parasol again, and Simon hastily sprang back.

"My deepest apologies, dear lady," he said. "I had, believe me, no intent to cause distress."

"I don't think we should be arguing," Alex said. "The way I understand it, the only way for us to get home again is to find what we're looking for while the Moon is still blue. Three days, more or less, before the way goes shut, the lady in the library said." How much time did they have left? he wondered. How long had he and Zeke and Tetley wandered around in that strange fog? "Maybe if we all stick together and help each other, we'll have a better chance."

"Good thought, lad," Simon said, gingerly rubbing his chest.

"Two heads are better than one," Miss

Mumsley said briskly, resettling her parasol. "And if that's true, four heads should be better yet. Five, counting this exceptional dog."

"Quite," Simon said. He squared his bony shoulders and straightened his velvet cap.

"And I've had quite enough of this Moon," Miss Mumsley said, snapping her parasol open and raising it over her head. "It seems a drab and dreadful place. I miss my garden. And I would like a hot bath."

"I miss ale," Simon said. "And fishing."

Tetley lowered his aviator goggles.

"This way, don't you think?" Miss Mumsley said. "Away from that horrible fog. Over there beyond the boulders I believe I see the beginning of a path."

CHAPTER 7

The Tollgate

*In which Alex and his companions
avoid the perils of willful waste*

There was a barrier across the path. It looked like the sort of swinging gate found in airport parking lots, put there to keep cars from sneaking through without paying a parking fee. A sign tacked to the gate read PAY TOLL in large spidery letters.

Tetley, Simon, Miss Mumsley, and Alex drew up in front of it, while Zeke snuffed busily around their feet. He had been rolling in moon dust, which made him look floury and blue.

"Locked right up, it is," said Tetley unhelpfully.

"The better to climb, my good rat," Simon said cheerily. "No lock holds back the resourceful adventurer. Balked of one path, the creative mind moves on to another."

"PAY TOLL," Miss Mumsley read in a puzzled voice. "What toll, do you suppose? And to whom?"

"Yoo-hoo!" a shrill voice screeched.

Simon, caught with one foot on the bottom rung of the gate, hastily got down. Zeke stopped snuffing and began to bark.

"Over here!"

The air was filled with a faint blue haze. The landscape of the moon spread out on either side of them, a strange empty desert that reminded Alex of gravel quarries and slag pits. Set among the rocks to the left of the path was a stone cottage with a stone porch across the front, and on the porch stood a woman dressed in black, beckoning and waving her arms.

"Over here!" the woman shrieked again. *"You have to pay the toll!"*

They stumbled toward her across the uneven ground. Simon hung back to murmur worriedly to Alex.

"Hast any money, lad?"

Alex shook his head.

"Nor do I," Simon said. "Not so much as a penny piece. Mayhap the lady . . . or yon *Rattus* . . ."

But Miss Mumsley and Tetley were no better off. Miss Mumsley was unfazed.

"We will explain our situation," she said. "We will tell her that we are merely visitors here who hope to be leaving soon and explain that we are severely pressed for time."

"And coins," Simon said.

"We will enlist her sympathies," Miss Mumsley said. "We are strangers in a strange land, penniless, and striving to return home. Our plight cannot fail to touch her heart."

As they drew closer to the cottage, however, Alex began to suspect with a sinking feeling that Miss Mumsley was wrong. The woman on the porch was dressed all in black, and had skinned-back black hair, flinty black eyes, thin lips that turned down at the corners, and a long neck that poked, vulturelike, out of a high black collar. At the sight of her, Zeke began to growl low in his throat.

"Stop it, Zeke," Alex said. "He won't hurt you," he added hastily.

The woman gave a nasty-sounding laugh.

"I'd like to see him try," she said. She had a scratchy voice like a crow. She made a strange flicking motion with her fingers, and Zeke stopped growling and put his tail between his legs.

The woman regarded the little group with a greedy eye, then pointed abruptly at Alex and beckoned.

"Toll, please!" she said.

Alex fumbled hopelessly in his coinless pockets.

"How much is it?" he asked.

"Not how much, but what and why," the woman cawed back. "Willful waste makes woeful want, and if you can't pay the toll, you'll have to serve your time until you do. Like him."

She pointed with a long clawlike finger. They all turned their heads.

Slumped in a chair in a far corner of the porch was a man wearing an elaborate wig and a broad-brimmed hat covered with curly plumes. He looked as if he were dressed for a costume ball, in a long-skirted emerald brocade coat, satin knee breeches, and high-heeled shoes with jeweled buckles. There were glittering rings on his fingers and gold lace at his throat and wrists.

"Greetings, good sir!" Simon called out, but the elegant man made no response. He just sat, staring dully at nothing, his face set in lines of misery and despair.

"Too busy to chat, he is," the crow woman cackled gleefully. "He's hard at work now, wearing things out. A new coat and a pair of shoes a day, he had, and three fine linen shirts, all cast away when the day was over and new ones the next morning.

"'The Earl of Barnstaple, my good woman,' he said to me, looking down that long nose of his, 'does not wear the same garment twice.'

"'Willful waste makes woeful want,' I said. 'Use it up, wear it out, make do, or here you sit until you pay the toll.'

"And there he sits, wearing out, with another fine suit to go when that one's finished, and then another and another. Offered me his jeweled buckles, he did, but that's no toll, I said, not by my reckoning."

She pointed a skinny finger at Miss Mumsley.

"Willful waste brings woeful want!" the crow woman shrieked. "For want of a nail, the shoe was lost! A penny saved is a penny earned! See a pin and pick it up; all the day you'll have good luck! See a pin and let it lay; bad luck you'll have all the day! A stitch in time saves nine!"

She threw the cottage door open and pointed toward the room inside.

"Pay the toll or serve your time!"

Alex and Miss Mumsley leaned forward, and Simon stood on tiptoe to peer over their heads. In the center of the room sat a girl with long yellow braids and a furious expression. She was mending a long tear in what looked like a bed sheet or an enormous tablecloth, and she was crying as she sewed. The white cloth was spotted with blood where she had pricked her fingers. A basket beside her was heaped with piles and piles of torn and tattered clothes.

"My dear, what are you doing?" Miss Mumsley called, but the yellow-haired girl acted as if she hadn't heard. She continued stitching and angrily crying, with her head bent close to her work as if the tears were making it hard to see.

"This is outrageous!" Miss Mumsley protested. "What could that poor girl have done to be treated like that?"

The crow woman pulled the cottage door closed, shutting the sobbing girl inside.

"Willful waste!" she chortled. "Wouldn't darn her stockings, she wouldn't, or sew on a button or patch a knee. Pay the toll or serve your time!"

Miss Mumsley thumped her parasol angrily on the porch floor.

"Well, at least you can't make *me* sew, you hideous woman!" she snapped.

She lifted her pink skirt to reveal a length of white cotton stocking, neatly darned across the ankle.

"I always do my mending! And when I see a pin"—she tore open her reticule and brandished a hairpin under the crow woman's nose—"I pick it up! And if you think you can keep us here, staring at the floor or stabbing at our fingers—"

The crow woman darted forward and snatched the hairpin out of her hand.

"Now *there's* a pretty toll," she cackled. "One paid, and very nicely too!"

As Miss Mumsley stared, her mouth open, the woman whirled again to point at Alex. "Willful waste makes woeful want! What about *you,* my fine boy?"

Alex dug wildly through his pockets. What would the willful waste woman take as a toll? What would she make him do if he didn't have anything she wanted?

He held out his findings on the palm of his hand. The woman bent over him, poking delicately through his possessions with a skinny finger. Three peppermint candies still in their wrappers, a Doggie Treat in a foil packet, a whistle on a cord, an eraser, a tin button on a pin from a trip to a museum. She flicked them aside, shaking her head.

"Pay the toll or serve your time," the crow woman cackled. "Now *I* save it all, I do: string and scraps and paper sacks, pennies, pins, and postage stamps, bottle caps and buttons, rubber bands and cherry pits. All your throwaways come here for me to care for, and a wasteful lot you are indeed. Use it up; wear it out."

Alex felt his heart sink. He'd been wasteful and now he was going to pay for it by spending years and years picking up pins or doing something else hateful.

"Look again, lad!" It was Simon. "Surely you have something to satisfy yon beldame. Look again!"

The crow woman cackled greedily.

Alex desperately thrust his hands deep into his emptied pockets. There *was* something else there. Something small and lumpy caught in the seam at the very bottom of the pocket. He tugged at it, but it stuck.

The crow woman watched him impatiently, tapping her foot on the porch floor. Her shoe was patched and repatched and tied with shoelaces that had been broken and knotted over and over again.

He tugged at the lumpy something again, finally jerking it free. Hardly daring to look at it, he pulled it out. It was a pencil stub.

There was just the barest bit of yellow pencil left between sharpened point and rubbed eraser. Alex couldn't think why he'd saved it. It was too small to write with. But the willful waste woman pounced upon it as if it were a gold nugget.

"Now *that's* more like it," she cawed. "Two tolls paid, and the dog can pass for free. So that leaves you, young man, and the rat."

Simon reached confidently into the pouch that hung from the belt of his shabby robe.

"Now that I understand you, my good woman," he said, "I find I have no end of tolls. I am but a poor scholar, none of your wealthy lords or gold-shod city merchants. When one's resources are few, one wastes little. Here. Choose."

The contents of Simon's pouch proved that he, at least, was free of willful waste. He had three candle ends, burned to the last bare inch;

a length of twine, rolled tightly into a small ball; a torn scrap of parchment, folded; a linen hand-kerchief, patched; and a gnawed rind of cheese.

The crow woman snatched one of the candle ends, and then, scornfully, between the tips of two fingers, accepted one of Tetley's rusty nails.

"Three tolls paid, and four!" she cried. "All may pass! Willful waste makes woeful want!"

Clutching her handful of oddments as if they were treasures, she turned and scuttled into the cottage, closing the door firmly behind her. Alex turned to look toward the path.

"Look, the gate's swinging open," he said. "Let's go before she changes her mind."

Simon nodded.

"Let's waste no time in leaving," he said. "By Saint Bruno's bootstraps, that lady made my blood run cold. A face and form like a carrion crow."

"Just a moment," Miss Mumsley said.

She bustled past them, holding her skirts in both hands, and hurried up the steps and along the porch to bend over the motionless man in emerald brocade. She shook him by the shoulder.

"Hurry!" she whispered, glancing anxiously toward the closed cottage door. "She's gone inside. You can come with us, away from here. But we have to hurry!"

The man said nothing. He shook his head—the barest movement—and slumped lower in his chair, eyes on nothing, the gold lace of his sleeves sweeping the porch floor.

"Come on!" Miss Mumsley urged, louder. She prodded him with her parasol. "Quickly! Why won't you *listen?* Have a little gumption!"

"Bestir yourself, man!" called Simon.

Alex looked worriedly toward the tollgate. It was fully open now, leaving the path clear.

"We have to go," he said.

"Unless you has more tolls," said Tetley.

Miss Mumsley tried one more prod, then reluctantly hurried to join them, glancing back unhappily over her shoulder at the motionless form in emerald brocade.

The tollgate was slowly swinging shut again. Together they rushed toward it and dashed through.

CHAPTER 8

The Lozar

In which there is a picnic,
a catastrophe, and a battle

They paused to rest at a circle of smooth rocks
a short distance off the path. The rocks were
sprinkled with tiny flecks of silver and crystal
that made them glitter, and they were flat on
top. Four smaller rocks sat around a larger slab
in the middle, looking, Alex thought, like park
benches around a picnic table. The only thing
missing was something to eat.

Alex's stomach was growling. He was hungry

enough to eat the artificial cherries on Miss Mumsley's hat. Glumly he passed around the three peppermint candies—one each for himself, Simon, and Miss Mumsley—and unwrapped the Doggie Treat for Zeke. Simon gave Tetley his rind of cheese.

Zeke, who had eaten both his treat and its foil wrapper, pranced away from the picnic rocks to run in circles through the moondust. Occasionally he paused, barking excitedly, to pounce at something invisible on the ground and then run forward in pursuit of it.

"A fine animal," Simon said.

"I had a cat," Miss Mumsley said wistfully. "I hope she's still all right, back home. She was such a dear. Her name was Piccalilli."

"Cats is bad," Tetley said direfully, nose in his cheese rind.

"They are not," said Miss Mumsley.

"Are too," said Tetley.

"It is not fit, good rat, to contradict a lady," said Simon.

"Is too," said Tetley.

"He's getting too far away," Alex said.

He raised his voice. "Zeke! Here, boy!"

Some distance away, clouds of dust arose where Zeke was gleefully digging a hole. At Alex's shout, he stopped digging and began to run teasingly back and forth, ears flapping, tongue hanging out.

"Zeke!" Alex shouted again.

"I smell something," Miss Mumsley said suddenly, wrinkling her nose. "Something . . . fetid."

Alex sniffed the blue air. Miss Mumsley was right. There was a dank smell of mold and dark cellars. A smell that reminded Alex queasily of something that had been a long time buried.

Tetley, trembling, gave a terrified squeak and put his hubcap over his head.

"It's a Time Eater, see?" he said in a quavering voice.

Miss Mumsley and Simon got hastily to their feet.

"What is a Time Eater?" Miss Mumsley asked, looking confusedly behind her.

With a jolt of alarm, Alex remembered what the Moon Rats had said.

"They eat time," he said urgently. "*Your* time.

They just suck it up like vampires until there isn't any of it left. And then nothing is left of *you* either. Nothing but a husk, the Moon Rats said."

Miss Mumsley took a step backward and turned pale.

"Time," Simon said, lifting a finger. He was wearing his dazed faraway look again. "Time, too, is never-ending. Second after second, minute after minute, year after year, it goes on and on and on and—"

"Not *now*, Mr. Nash!" Miss Mumsley said sharply.

She prodded the quivering Tetley with her parasol.

"How do we protect ourselves from this vile creature?" she demanded.

"Zeke!" Alex shouted frantically. *"Zeke!"*

The dead smell grew stronger.

"The beast stinks of graveyard dirt," Simon said.

Then they saw it.

It stepped out from behind a great blue boulder, a tall dark creature wrapped in shadow. It wore a long shapeless garment with a cowled hood that hid its face and flowing skirts that dragged in the blue dust. Deep inside the hood's darkness there was a glittering pinpoint flicker of eyes.

Miss Mumsley gave a little gasp of dismay, but stood her ground.

"Who are you?" she demanded in a high unnatural-sounding voice. "What do you want?"

The Time Eater's voice was a shivery hiss that made Alex's flesh crawl and the hair stand up on the back of his neck.

"I am the Lozar," it whispered.

> *"Lord and lady, lad and lass,*
> *One and all are in my grasp,*
> *Grazing cow and rooting swine,*
> *Flock and farmer, all are mine.*
> *Beggar, baron, tinker, tailor,*
> *Fool and scholar, soldier, sailor,*
> *Babe and mother, dog and steed,*
> *All I gather—and I feed."*

Simon strode forward, grasped Miss Mumsley by the elbow, thrust her firmly behind him, and pointed a trembling finger in the direction of the Time Eater's chin.

"Begone, foul demon!" he ordered in a choked voice. "In the name of all the holy saints!"

The Time Eater shook back its sleeve to reveal a withered gray-blue hand. It crooked its fingers in a beckoning gesture as it moved steadily closer over the dusty ground, first turning toward Miss Mumsley, then toward Simon, and finally toward Alex.

"I hunger," it whispered. "I come to gather time."

Alex tried to move, to dart to where Simon and Miss Mumsley stood behind the picnic rock, but his feet were frozen to the ground. There was a roaring in his ears, and the scene before his eyes began to spin and blur. The Time Eater drifted closer. As if from a great distance, Alex could hear Simon and Miss Mumsley shouting his name.

Then everything snapped back into focus. Zeke, frantically barking, galloped furiously toward them, kicking up great clouds of dust, and sprang upon the Time Eater from the rear.

The Time Eater twisted like smoke. Zeke

growled once fiercely, and then the creature was upon him, winding its arms around him and digging its bony fingers into his fur. It bent its shadowed face toward Zeke's neck. Zeke gave a strangled shriek and began to thrash.

Alex didn't stop to think.

He hurled himself ferociously at the Time Eater's hunched back, screaming and flailing wildly with his fists.

"Leave him alone!" he shrieked. *"Leave him alone!"*

The Time Eater barely seemed to notice. It twisted again and slithered away, dragging Zeke with it. Zeke was moaning now and his paws dragged limply in the dust.

"Unhand yon hound!" Simon bellowed. He plunged past Alex, seized the Time Eater by the shoulder, and jerked violently upward. But again the creature twisted bonelessly out of his grasp. It seemed to be fastened to Zeke like a leech.

"Drop that dog, you miserable wretch!" Miss Mumsley screeched, forcing her way into the fray.

She jabbed at the Time Eater viciously with

the point of her parasol, then drew back and jabbed again. This seemed to have some effect. The Time Eater paused in its feeding and lifted its head. As it did, Tetley brought his hubcap down with a resounding crash.

The Time Eater shuddered and hissed. Then, with a wriggling motion like an eel, it flickered under their arms and slid rapidly away. It straightened when it was well out of reach and paused looking back at them, turning facelessly from one to the other.

"I am the Lozar," it whispered. "We will meet again."

Then it turned and paced unhurriedly away, finally rounding a boulder and disappearing, shadow blending with shadow, into a patch of hovering mist.

They stood looking after it in horror. Miss Mumsley sat down abruptly on a rock.

"I hit it, I did," Tetley said in an astonished voice, hugging his hubcap.

"That was very well done of you, Tetley," Miss Mumsley said. "What a hideous creature. How is the dog? Is he all right?"

"He's yet alive," Simon answered, but he sounded unhappy.

Zeke was alive, but the Time Eater's feeding had done its work. He had aged before their eyes. His glossy golden-brown coat had turned gray. An ancient dog lay there, eyes faded and dim. His ribs stood out beneath his rough fur, one ear drooped, and when he struggled tiredly to his feet, he limped pitifully as if something hurt his paws. He nuzzled Alex forlornly and whimpered. Alex threw his arms around him. He wanted to burst into tears.

Simon patted his shoulder.

"It's not your fault, lad," he said gently.

Alex shook his head. *It is my fault,* he thought bitterly. *This wouldn't have happened if we had just stayed at home. The Time Eater should have taken me, not Zeke.*

Miss Mumsley got to her feet and shook out the skirts of her rose-colored dress.

"We're *not* going to put up with this," she said angrily. "Savage an innocent animal, would they? Well, not while I have breath in *my* body. *I,* I'll have you know, am the chapter head of the Picketsville Society for the Prevention of Cruelty to Animals, and we simply do not put up with this sort of thing! Even this abominable place must have some sense of fair play and moral decency. We're not going to take this lying down. We're going to make them pay!"

"But how?" Alex asked. "What can *we* do?"

"I don't know yet," Miss Mumsley said. "But we'll think of something."

She tucked her parasol firmly under her arm and straightened her hat. Then she reached down and gently stroked Zeke's drooping ear.

"Come on, old boy," she said softly. "Let's get back on the path. You walk with me for a bit. Come along, Tetley. Alex, Mr. Nash. Let's be off."

"By Saint Gertrude's garters, that's a brave and gallant lady," Simon said to Alex, behind Miss Mumsley's rose-colored back.

"And a fair damsel too," he added.

But when Alex turned to ask him what he meant, Simon was studying something in the distance and his ears had turned as pink as Miss Mumsley's parasol.

CHAPTER 9

The Gallery of Ar

*In which Alex and his companions
meet a Musician*

They had been walking for what felt like hours.

Miss Mumsley, still stalking majestically in the lead, was murmuring words of encouragement to a weary Zeke. Alex could hardly bear to watch him, limping so painfully through the blue dust. His own feet hurt too. Tetley had begun to drag his hubcap wearily along the ground, and Simon, who had been whistling bravely, was now humming something tuneless and dismal that sounded like a funeral dirge.

Then the path before them turned sharply to the right through a tunnel in a tumbled pile of enormous blue boulders. When they emerged, they found themselves face-to-face with an impressive building made of gleaming white stone. There were carved white pillars across the front and a wide front door studded with shiny star-shaped nails. The building looked off-balance somehow, and after a moment Alex figured out what the trouble was. There were three pillars on one side of the door and only two on the other.

"What on earth . . . ?" began Miss Mumsley.

Simon pointed to the name engraved over the front door.

"'The Gallery of Ar,'" he read, frowning. "An odd world, this. Who or what is Ar?"

"I don't know," Miss Mumsley said, gathering up her skirts and sweeping up the marble steps. "But I'm going to find out. Perhaps they have some food and drink and a place to sit down."

She rapped sharply on the front door with her parasol.

The door was flung open by a man in the oddest costume Alex had seen yet. He wore a green velvet beret with a peacock feather in it, a belted purple smock that came to his knees, blue-and-yellow striped leggings, and a pair of curly-toed scarlet leather shoes. Long yellow curls hung to his shoulders, a small pointed beard jutted from the end of his chin, and under one arm he carried a strange stringed instrument. Alex had never seen anything like it before. It looked a bit like a small guitar and a bit like a flattened pumpkin.

"A lute!" Simon exclaimed. "And a troubador, as I live and breathe!"

The man in the doorway gave a bow so deep that his feather swept the floor.

"Welcome, honored guests, to the Gallery of Ar," he said. "I am Sebastian the Musician, entirely at your service. Enter, enter, my lords and lady, to view the marvels within. We have paintings in watercolor and oils; posters, prints, and pastel works; drawings in charcoal, crayon, and India ink; sculptures in stone, ceramic, and papier-mâché; and an incomparable collection of musical scores and poetic effusions, all displayed to suit the most discerning artistic eye."

He swung the door open wider and gestured grandly with his free hand.

"Enter, enter!" he repeated grandly. "Feast your eyes upon the marvelous sights about to be before you!"

"We were hoping," Miss Mumsley said dampingly, "to perhaps feast upon something a little more substantial. We are tired, hungry, and thirsty, and this dog is old and ill. Do you by chance have anything to eat or drink? And a comfortable place where we could sit and rest for a short time?"

Sebastian's expression became peevish.

"No food or drink is allowed in the Gallery," he said sternly.

Then he brightened.

"But we do have some most realistic paintings of banquets, with a roast duck or two, and an attractive still life of boiled fish with onions on a platter. And some refreshing landscape scenes with streams and rivers, and a charming portrait of children drawing water from a well."

He looked so eager that Alex felt sorry for him. He tugged at Simon's sleeve.

"After all, we're here," he muttered. "We should at least take a look."

"I confess to some curiosity," admitted Simon. "Aye, lad, let us have a look inside. The dog can sleep a bit on yon porch, and perhaps, if we do not offend this Sebastian, he will tell us where we can find a spot of meat and ale."

He strode forward and offered Miss Mumsley his arm. After a moment of hesitation, Miss Mumsley took it, and the two of them followed the Musician into the Gallery. Alex and Tetley trailed behind them, Alex reluctantly looking back to where Zeke lay asleep on the porch, his gray head pillowed tiredly on his sore paws.

The inside of the Gallery was a vast marble hall, its walls thickly hung with paintings. Glass cases were scattered about in the center of the floor, and there were statues on pedestals in alcoves. Sebastian scampered excitedly ahead of them, calling back over his shoulder and gesturing with his lute at objects they should be sure not to miss.

Simon and Miss Mumsley stopped to peer into one of the glass cases, while Alex and Tetley headed toward a display of statuary. Alex wanted to get a better look at those statues. There was something funny about them.

"His head's stuck, it is," Tetley said as they drew closer.

It wasn't stuck exactly, Alex reflected. It just wasn't there.

The statue showed the bottom half of a noble Roman in sandals and a draped toga. Above the waist, though, there was nothing but a blank block of stone. The statue had never been finished. On the pedestal beside it perched a carved horse, its head and forefeet sticking uncomfortably out of an uncut chunk of rock.

"Horse's bottom's stuck," Tetley said, snickering hysterically.

"They're not finished," Alex said. "None of them are finished."

The paintings were no better. There were landscapes with no land and seascapes with no sea and portraits with no faces and forest scenes with white splotchy places that were clearly supposed to have been trees.

"Nothing's finished," Alex said again.

A thought suddenly struck him.

"Even the *name* isn't finished," he said. "The Gallery of *Ar*. But I'll bet it's supposed to be *Art*. *Art*. With a *t* on the end."

"Precisely!" Sebastian said, materializing suddenly from behind a pedestal that held the right half of a Civil War general. "None of it is finished! And a good thing too! An unfinished work of art is still alive with possibilities. But once it's done—once that final stroke of paint has been applied, that final chip of stone chiseled, that final note sounded—why, then it's all over. Finished. Finalized. Dead. But *these* that you see around you"—he gestured triumphantly with his lute—"*these* are works in progress! The true breathing essence of creation!"

Alex looked in the direction of the pointing lute and saw a gold-framed painting of half a basket containing half a kitten.

"But . . ." he began doubtfully.

"I myself," Sebastian said, "*never* finish a piece."

He struck a chord on the lute and burst suddenly into song.

> *"Oh, early in the morning*
> *When birds were first winging,*
> *I heard a young maiden*
> *Who sweetly was—"*

He stopped abruptly.

"Singing," said Tetley, looking pleased with himself.

"No, no." Sebastian shook his head.

Tetley looked sullen.

"Is too," he said.

"Oh, no. It *could* be *singing,* of course, but it might also be *ringing*—with a bell, you know—or *swinging,* on a swing. Or she could be *bringing* something somewhere. Or even *kinging.* If she were playing checkers, you see. The point is that it isn't finished. It's still ripe with potential."

"Things that doesn't get *finished*," Tetley said ominously, "doesn't *work*."

"Come see this!" Miss Mumsley called.

She was bending over a case in the middle of the floor, tapping a finger on the glass.

"Mr. Beethoven's Unfinished Symphony," she said. "And look at this."

It was a yellowed sheet of paper with a few scribbled lines of poetry. The poem ended abruptly in the middle of the page and was followed by the word *PORLOCK* written over and over again in angry capital letters. At one point the writer had stabbed his pen right through the page.

"What is it?" Alex asked. "I can't read it. The handwriting is awful."

"It's an unfinished poem by a poet named Samuel Taylor Coleridge," Miss Mumsley said. "It's quite famous. He was interrupted in the middle of it by a person from Porlock pounding on his door and afterward he was never able to remember what he had been about to say. And here it is. What there is of it."

"We have an extensive collection of unfinished literary works." Sebastian appeared, nodding brightly, at Miss Mumsley's elbow. "Compositions by poets unable to find a rhyme for *chalcedony* or *anthropomorphism,* for example, or manuscripts by mystery writers unable to follow their own clues—why, there's a whole room in the back for unfinished novels alone. Some of them are hardly even started. There's nothing more than a *The* on the page, or a *Once upon a time.*"

"A pity we won't have time to see them," Miss Mumsley said firmly. "But we really must be on our way. Could you tell us where we might be able to find a meal? Somewhere close by?"

Sebastian looked crestfallen.

"There is an establishment," he said unwillingly. "It's not far. If you just keep on the path in the direction that you were going, you can hardly miss it."

"Thank you, Sebastian," Miss Mumsley said. "We've had quite a delightful time. Are you ready, Alex? Tetley? Where's Mr. Nash?"

Simon was discovered on the opposite side of the hall behind a statue of Saint George and the Dragon. Saint George, unfinished below the waist, was poking his sword into an unformed lump from which protruded a scaly tail.

"I have come upon a treasure coffer," Simon said. "You should hardly leave it so," he said severely to Sebastian. "We are all honest folk, but who knows who next may pass this way? Thieves, murderers, or brigands, mayhap. And a king's ransom sitting here uncovered, ripe for the plucking."

They crowded around, eager for a glimpse of the treasure.

Simon had found a massive carved chest with the top thrown carelessly back, filled to brimming with glittering gold and silver coins.

"Wow," Alex said.

"Goodness," Miss Mumsley said, staring. "Wherever did you get it?"

"Oh, those," Sebastian said. "They're talents. You doubtless have plenty of your own. Most people find that they do, if they just take the time to search them out."

"Talents?" Alex said blankly.

"*Wasted* talents," Sebastian said. "Talents their owners never bothered to discover, or discovered but never bothered to use. They're all in here."

He poked his lute disgustedly at the treasure chest.

"Talents for everything from clarinet-playing to croquet, tennis to trigonometry, bubble-blowing to ballet. Talents for walking on your hands or reciting things backward or wiggling your ears. And wasted, every one."

Tetley, frowning effortfully, began to wiggle his ears.

"I don't think it's fair to say all those talents are *wasted*," Alex said. "I mean, you can't really waste something if you never even know it's there."

"It's obvious that it's *there*," the Musician said crossly. "But it takes effort to figure out what it *is*. That's the tricky part. You have to try things out."

He seized a handful of coins and tossed

them into the air, watching them fall in a golden shower.

"Lazy, that's what I call it," he said.

Miss Mumsley tried to thank him again for his hospitality, but he waved her words away.

"Well, goodbye," he said. "Good luck. Stop by again if you're in the neighborhood."

As they reached the path, he shouted after them, waving his lute in the air.

"Don't forget to use your talents! And remember that true art is always a work in progress!"

"Interesting," Miss Mumsley said. "But most peculiar."

"Horse's bottom," Tetley said.

CHAPTER 10

Dinner at the Moondust Café

In which a very strange meal
is not quite shared

That must be it," said Alex, pointing into the distance. "The establishment Sebastian told us about. It looks like a diner. I mean a place to eat," he hurriedly explained, seeing their blank expressions. "He said we wouldn't be able to miss it."

"I should think not," Miss Mumsley said.

The establishment was a long, low, silver-colored building on wheels topped by an enormous flashing neon sign. The sign showed a blinking moon in electric blue. Beside it in sizzling pink letters were the words THE MOONDUST CAFÉ. Every few minutes the pink letters turned into little bursts of gold sparks and disappeared, only to reappear again, pinker and brighter than ever.

"What manner of magic is this?" demanded Simon in an awestruck voice. "It looks like Greek fire, yet it never dims or burns out. How is this possible?"

Alex plunged into a confused explanation of electricity, only to be abruptly interrupted by Miss Mumsley.

"If we postpone our discussion and go inside," she said crisply, "the proprietor may provide us with something to eat."

Meekly they followed her up the metal steps and through the café door.

"Astonishing," Simon said.

"A lady who knows her own mind," he finished, seeing Alex's puzzled look.

From all around the dimly lit room, faces turned to look at them as they paused in the doorway. The café was full of people—and the oddest collection of people Alex had ever seen in his life.

There was a beautiful blonde woman in a long white robe sharing a booth with an immensely fat lady in purple. A pair of bearded men in slouch-brimmed hats leaned against the wall, next to heavy packs hung with bedrolls and mining tools; and a cluster of military officers, their chests loaded with gold braid and ribbons, huddled around a table in the middle of the floor. A knight in chain mail, his silk tabard embroidered with scarlet griffins, sprawled in the corner, drinking something out of a paper cup. Across from him, a dour-looking man in a top hat and a ruffled shirt was playing a game of solitaire.

They threaded their way through the throng and sat down at an empty table. They had barely settled themselves when a waitress appeared at Alex's elbow. She was wearing a ruffled apron and she was chewing gum.

"Welcome to the Moondust Café," she said. "How may I help you?"

"Food, lass, and drink," Simon said briskly, "and plenty of both. And a plate of tasty scraps for this fine dog."

The waitress scribbled on a pad. "Five specials," she said.

"And a cup of tea," put in Miss Mumsley.

"A mug of ale," added Simon.

"And a glass of milk, please," said Alex. "What about you, Tetley?"

Tetley shook his head. He was shaking a nearly empty ketchup bottle.

"Just a minute," Alex said to the waitress. "Is it always this crowded in here? Who are all these people?"

The waitress shrugged. "They come and go," she said. "The blonde—she's someone's lost muse. Can't get by without her, to hear her tell about it, but he doesn't seem in any hurry to come after her, if you ask me. And the one in purple—she's lost her voice. Or at least part of it. She's a prima donna, she says, and she's looking for her high C."

"An opera singer," Miss Mumsley murmured. "How sad."

"What about the soldiers?" Alex asked.

"Lost battles," the waitress said. "And those two with the pickaxes have lost their silver mine, and the dandy with the playing cards has lost his luck. And the knight—*he's* lost his lady's favor and no surprise, in my opinion, surly brute that he is." She stuffed her pad into the pocket of her apron.

"Back in a flash," she said.

She returned with a tray of cups and glasses, then disappeared again in the direction of the kitchen.

Miss Mumsley reached eagerly for her teacup, then drew back with a frown.

"This must be a mistake," she said. "There's nothing but the dregs here. And it's cold."

Simon set down his glass.

"And mine is nothing but froth and bubbles," he said, frowning.

Alex took a hesitant sip of his milk and made a horrible face.

"Mine is sour," he said. "It tastes awful."

The waitress reappeared and began unloading a tray of silverware and plates.

Simon put out a staying hand. "A moment, lass," he said. "This looks to me like another's meal." He pointed at the plate in front of him. It contained fish sticks, mashed potatoes, and peas. There were bites out of two of the fish sticks, and the potatoes were half eaten.

The waitress dropped a handful of forks and spoons in the middle of the table.

"It's the special," she said. "There's no point in complaining. We do our best, considering what we have to work with. Leftovers, that's all we get. All the bits left behind by those who don't clean their plates. Plenty of sandwich crusts and spinach, but look what they send us for dessert."

She gestured bitterly toward the plates on her tray.

"Nothing but crumbs. Sometimes a pudding that didn't set comes in, or a batch of burned cookies, but otherwise we just have to make do. It's a terrible way to run a business."

She set a plate of fish sticks on the floor for Zeke and left.

Alex prodded distastefully at his fish sticks.

"Is there any ketchup yet?" he asked Tetley.

Tetley gave the bottle a final tremendous shake. The cap flew off, and ketchup spurted across the table.

"No," Tetley said.

"Mine is overcooked," Miss Mumsley said after a moment. "And oversalted."

Simon crammed a fish stick into his mouth.

"It could be far worse," he said cheerily, chewing. "At least there are no maggots."

Miss Mumsley winced, but managed an approving nod.

"You set an excellent example, Mr. Nash," she said. "Not everyone has your fortitude when faced with trouble."

She glanced unhappily at the prospectors, and Alex suspected she was thinking of the vanished Jeremiah Stone.

The waitress returned to collect their plates, bringing with her two cups of cold coffee, a bowl of melted ice cream, and a gnawed brownie. She thumped the bill down on the table, but shook her head at Alex's worried look.

"It's just a formality," she said. "All the unpaid bills end up here too. Terrible way to run a business," she repeated.

"Could I ask a question?" Miss Mumsley said. "We—my companions and I—are looking for a lost heart, a lost way, and lost time. If you, perhaps, had any suggestions . . ."

The waitress pursed her lips, frowning.

"For the lost heart, I'd try the Crystal Forest," she said. "Just stay on the road and you'll see it, off to the left. The lost way—for that you'll want the Pointless Tower. And as for the lost time— well, that would be the Norns, I'd say, but if I were you, I'd keep well away. Scary those old women are, with their spinning and their snipping, and not a care for nobody but themselves."

"Old women?" Alex repeated.

But the waitress had bustled away.

He turned, puzzled, to the others. "What did she mean about old women? Spinning?"

"She meant don't go near they," Tetley said firmly, licking ketchup off his whiskers.

Miss Mumsley reached across the table and patted Alex's hand.

"Don't worry about it," she said. "I'm sure you'll figure it out. Perhaps we'll meet someone more knowledgeable along the way."

"Time we were off," Simon said, getting grandly to his feet.

CHAPTER 11

The Norn

*In which information is acquired from
a stranger by the side of the road*

The Crystal Forest was farther than the waitress had implied. There was no sign of it in sight and night was falling. The Moon's blue light was growing steadily dimmer. They trudged on in the gathering dusk, their shadows—impossibly long, thin, and navy blue—shooting out eerily before them.

Then suddenly a voice spoke out of the dark.

"And who might you be, my lords and lady,

and where might you be going, all in the gloaming?"

Tetley squeaked, Miss Mumsley gave a little shriek, and Alex nearly jumped out of his skin. Nothing could be seen of the speaker but a shadowy shape huddled in a shawl. Something flashed in her fingers, moving rapidly up and down like a yo-yo. Alex moved a step closer. It was an old woman, spinning. A long luminous thread grew from her twirling spindle, rising and falling in the misty dark.

"Not lords, I fear, good mistress, but simple commoners seeking a place to spend the night," said Simon with a little bow. "I am Simon Nash, scholar, and the lady is Miss Edith Mumsley of the land of Ohio. The lad is called Alex, the rat is Tetley, and this ancient dog, a sorry tale himself, is Zeke. And who might we have the honor of addressing?"

The woman gave a rusty little laugh and bent to fumble in a basket at her feet. As Alex's eyes grew more accustomed to the dimness, he could see that the basket was filled with spindles and tangled coils of yarn. Some of the strands were dull gray, but some glimmered with faint colors and a few were shot with startling gleams of gold.

"Ah, here they are," the woman said. "Yours, Mr. Nash, a good serviceable brown, but it's coming along, it is, and getting brighter by the minute."

She pulled a piece of yarn from the basket and dangled it before them. Alex caught a glimpse, before it dropped back into the mass, of a long thread of deep brown touched at the top with a growing stripe of glimmering rose.

"And yours, Miss Edith, you've had a gray stretch but you're doing up nicely now, and quite an interesting pattern it's turning into."

She tugged at the tangle in the basket and produced a pale pink thread that shaded into charcoal gray, then rose pink again, brighter than ever, interlaced with shimmery sparkles of copper brown.

"Very nice indeed," the old woman said. "Now *yours*"—she pointed an accusing finger at Alex—"has gotten into a bit of a tangle, and *his*"—she pointed at Zeke—"*his* is nearly broken off altogether. You'd think my sister had been at it, but she says no, when she snips a thread, she snips it clean."

Alex's heart lurched.

"Does I have a thread?" Tetley asked.

The woman gave a rusty chuckle. "Everyone has a thread, my dear, everyone. But yours isn't here. For rats, I have a different basket." She pursed her lips and shook her head. "And a sad snarl it is, my dears, all safety pins, string, and glue, though the threads hang together well enough."

"I don't understand," Alex said. "*Why* does everyone have a thread? What are they? Why is Zeke's broken? And why is mine all tangled?"

"Ah, my little lord, why indeed?" the old woman chuckled mockingly. "These are the threads of time, my dear, spinning out from year to year, one thread for each one of you, until my sister comes with her silver scissors to snip them free. And as to why yours is in a tangle, why, that's for you to find out, not for me.

You're the one as shapes the thread, my dear. All I do is spin."

Alex suddenly remembered the waitress at the Moondust Café. Scary old women with their spinning and snipping, she had said. He gasped and his eyes widened.

"Are you a Norn?"

The old woman dropped the spindle into the basket and gathered her shawl more closely around her head and shoulders.

"That I am, my dear, but no need to fear *me*, for the time here in my basket is time that was and time that is. Your danger comes from those who seek to seize time yet to be."

"Like the Lozar," Alex said.

The old woman nodded.

"Use your head, my boy, and all may yet come right." The old woman's voice was fading, and she was fading too, sinking deeper and deeper into the shadowed night. "I do hate a tangle," she said, her voice faraway and tiny.

"Wait!" Alex cried. "Don't go!"

But the Norn was gone.

Alex took a deep breath.

"There is safety pins in my thread," said Tetley in a resentful voice.

"At least yours isn't all tangled," Alex said. "Yours hangs together, she said. Mine is just a mess."

And Zeke's is almost broken through, he thought with a pang. It didn't bear thinking about.

"I don't see why it's a tangle," Miss Mumsley said. "I think you do very well."

"I think it all has something to do with my lost time," Alex said.

"How's that, lad?" Simon asked.

Alex tried to explain.

"Once I started really *thinking* about time," he said, "everything just got more and more muddled. I mean, you've only got so much time and it just keeps speeding past you. So why bother doing all this stuff? Like at school, learning the names of all the different kinds of clouds. What's that *for,* anyway? Or the parts of a butterfly. What difference does it make? Pretty soon all your time is going to be used up and your life is going to be over. So what's the point of doing *anything*? I mean, why bother?"

Simon, trudging beside him, was silent for so long that Alex began to think he hadn't been listening.

"Aye, lad, I see what you say," he said finally. "And it's fair true that each man—or woman," he added hastily, with a glance at Miss Mumsley, "has only so much time and not a jot longer. But just because one's time must end seems to me no reason to scorn what we've been given. There's time enough for living, Alexander, but each of us must choose how best to spend that time. And for me, it's the learning makes it all worthwhile. It's learning, lad, that makes the world a bigger place. Without it, we just crawl about like moles, seeing no more than the tunnel in front of our noses."

"We do?" Alex said.

Simon sighed.

"We do," he said. "And I begin to see my world as amazing small. Not like yours, with the fizzy electricity. I marvel thinking on it."

Alex found that he too had a lot to think about.

Tetley was still muttering about safety pins.

CHAPTER 12

The Inn of Abandoned Plans

*In which Alex and his companions
pass an eventful night*

There's a light up ahead," said Miss Mumsley,
sounding relieved.

They had been walking for some distance
since leaving the rock where they had met the
spinning woman, and it had been growing
darker all the time. They had passed no houses
or buildings at all, not even so much as a shel-
tering pile of boulders or stunted clump of trees.
Simon had begun speaking in a determinedly

cheerful, if somewhat strained, voice about the beauty of stars, the healthful benefits of night air, and the posture-enhancing advantages of hard sleeping surfaces.

Zeke was whimpering tiredly and dragging his paws.

"Just a little farther, boy," Alex whispered.

"A light," Miss Mumsley said again. "Perhaps they will be able to provide us with beds. Or at the very least, blankets."

"Indeed they will," said Simon as they drew nearer. "By Saint Cecilia's slippers, my lady, we have come to the right place."

The house was decidedly ramshackle. The roof sagged, the porch steps were broken, and pieces of cardboard were taped over places where there were missing windowpanes. But the illuminated sign over the front door read INN.

At the sight of it, Tetley began to titter.

"Instead of being OUT," he gurgled, "us will go INN. See? INN!"

He buried his face in his hubcap and giggled until he developed a fit of hiccups.

They cautiously mounted the rickety steps

and knocked on the front door, which promptly fell off its hinges. Nobody answered.

Simon knocked again—on the door frame this time—and bellowed, "Ho! Landlord! There are guests arrived!"

There was a sound of something (or someone) falling downstairs, ending in a heavy thump, and a moment later the landlord arrived, out of breath. He was plump, pink-faced, and bald, and he reminded Alex irresistibly of a round pink rubber ball. He was wearing a sweater with one arm missing. An elaborate pattern of triangles and leaping green deer stretched halfway across the chest and then faded out as if the knitter had despaired and given up. It gave him a peculiar lopsided look.

He bounced excitedly in the doorway, bobbing up and down on his toes, and panted, "Welcome! Welcome, privileged guests, to the Inn of Abandoned Plans! I am Jonathan Periwinkle, your evening's host! Enter! Enter!"

Then he turned and bawled back over his shoulder, *"Minerva! Prepare the bedchambers!"*

Simon bowed politely. "Indeed, good Master

Periwinkle, we do seek lodging for the night, but I fear that our financial situation . . ."

The landlord waved him aside.

"No, no, think nothing of it," he rumbled cheerfully. "You simply *intend* to pay, you see, but abandon the plan the next morning. Come right in, come right in. Sit down here in the sitting room, and Minerva will see that your beds are ready. Just a few minutes she'll be, as I can see you're all tired and in need of a rest. While you're waiting, let me fetch you something hot to drink."

He turned and bounded exuberantly out of the room. They could hear him bawling *"Minerva!"* as he receded down the passageway.

Tetley was still hiccupping.

"Hold your breath, Tetley, and count to one hundred," Miss Mumsley said severely.

"This is a weird room," Alex said. "Everything in it is falling apart."

The sitting room was just as dilapidated as the outside of the inn. The chairs and tables all had broken legs and were propped up awkwardly on boxes. There was a half-finished hooked rug on the floor, in a blobby pattern of polka dots, and a row of withered plants in pots stood on the mantelpiece.

"What are all those papers on the walls?" Miss Mumsley asked.

The walls of the sitting room were covered with curling sheets of dusty paper in different shapes and sizes, all covered with handwriting.

"They is *lists*," Tetley said, peering closer. "They is lists of things to do, see?"

He hiccupped loudly.

"Hold your breath again, Tetley," Miss Mumsley said.

"Unfinished lists," Simon said. "This one is all about planting cabbages. But it's only half checked off."

"This is some kid's homework assignments," Alex said. "She didn't do her arithmetic."

"'Letters to Write,'" Miss Mumsley read. "'Aunt Clara about the picnic basket, check. Cousin Arnold about the piglets, check.' But whoever it was never wrote Cousin Rose about the chocolate or Uncle William about the bicycle bell."

"Some of these are *old*," Alex said. "Listen to this one. 'Burnish ye helmete, check. Mende ye lefte gauntlet, check. Repaint ye escutcheon, three leopardes rampant and two bars, vermilion, check.' But then there's a whole bunch of other stuff unchecked."

"Preparing for a joust, it seems," Simon said, reading over his shoulder. "He seems to have gone ill equipped, poor lad."

"'To Pack for the Journey to the Colonies,'" read Miss Mumsley. "'Seed corn, one bag, check. Vegetable seeds, ten packets, check. Bolt of strong linen cloth, check. Goat'—oh, dear."

There was a scuffle of feet at the doorway, and the landlord entered, bearing a tray of steaming mugs.

"Ah, I see you have been examining the exhibits," he said, beaming, as he offered the mugs around.

"Extremely interesting," Miss Mumsley said.

Mr. Periwinkle gave a delighted nod. "They're all here," he said proudly. "Every abandoned plan, failed endeavor, discarded interest, and quashed quest." He pointed to a bookcase against the wall. "Books that people started but never finished," he said. "All with the original bookmarks."

He waved a hand at the mantelpiece.

"Houseplants that people neglected to water. And that map there, on the far wall"—he pointed to a faded map in a frame, stuck full of colored pins—"that's marked with all the places people planned to visit but never went to. We have stamp albums that never got filled with stamps, scrapbooks that never got filled with clippings, diaries dropped in the middle, unfinished airplane models, and ships that wouldn't fit in their bottles. And then, of course"—he rubbed his hands together gleefully, then pulled an enormous jar out from behind a broken rocking chair—"there are *these*."

They stared blankly at the jar. It seemed to be full of little lozenges of colored glass.

"What are they?" Alex asked. "They look like squished marbles."

"These, young sir, are good intentions," Mr. Periwinkle said impressively. "Good intentions that never came to anything. Good deeds that died before coming to fruition. Thank-you notes people never got around to writing, kind words they never bothered to speak, helping hands that never got offered. They all end up here."

He unscrewed the lid of the jar, scooped up a handful of lozenges, and let them dribble through his fingers.

"Pretty, aren't they?" he said. "They don't last long though. Leave a good intention long enough and it just fades away. This lot will be all gone in a day or two."

He sighed and screwed the top back on the jar.

"You'll be wanting your beds, I daresay. We have a private chamber prepared for the lady, but you gentlemen will have to share."

Miss Mumsley insisted on keeping Zeke with her, saying that she was going to soak his sore paws in warm water. She was escorted to a bed-room at the end of the hall. Simon, Alex, and Tetley were shown to the room next door, which was furnished with a wobbly-looking canvas cot and twin beds propped precariously on stacks of bricks. The beds were covered with a pair of partially pieced quilts and the cot with a crocheted afghan with the crochet hooks still stuck in it. Alex thought they were the most beautiful beds he had ever seen. He fell asleep almost before his head touched the half-stuffed pillow.

He awoke sometime later with the feeling that something was wrong. Tetley, a motionless lump on the cot, had wound the afghan around his head and was hiccupping softly in his sleep. Simon was snoring. Everything else was quiet. Alex lay uneasily on his back, listening with all his might. The wrong feeling simply wouldn't go away. In fact, it was getting worse.

Then, from outside the window, he heard a soft measured shuffle of footsteps. Someone was walking around outside. Alex held his breath.

Shuff—shuff—shuff. The slow footsteps drew closer and stopped. Someone was standing just outside the window. Alex could see a dark shapeless shadow through the dusty glass. The shadow raised its hand and pressed it against the glass. Then it began to scrape at the edges of the window frame as if looking for a way to get in.

Alex's heart gave a painful jolt in his chest. He was too scared to move.

Suddenly there was a thud and a scrabble of paws on the boards of the floor next door. Zeke was hurling himself against the walls, barking ferociously. Alex could hear the anxious murmur of Miss Mumsley's voice asking what was the matter. Then the bedroom door burst open and Zeke sprang furiously across the room toward the window, barking with all his might. The dark shadow pulled back and vanished.

Simon, in nothing but a voluminous linen shirt, leaped from the bed, shouting for a sword.

Alex ran to the window and peered out. The dark of night had lightened to a dim gray-blue light. Against it, Alex saw a tall dark shadow, just vanishing behind a mound of tumbled rocks. He sniffed experimentally and caught a faint whiff of dank-cellar smell, the odor Simon had described as graveyard dirt.

"My hiccups is gone," Tetley said.

Zeke, exhausted by his effort, nuzzled Alex's knee, then flopped down stiffly at his feet and put his head on his paws.

"You're a wonderful dog," Alex whispered, stroking his gray ears. His throat felt tight. "You're the best and bravest dog in the world."

"What's going on?" Miss Mumsley asked from the doorway. She was wrapped in another of the half-pieced quilts, with her bare feet and a bit of ruffled petticoat peeking out from beneath the patchwork. Her hair, which she had let down for the night, hung down the middle of her back and curled in little tendrils around her face. When she caught Simon staring at her, she blushed.

"Something was at the window," Alex said. "I think it was a Time Eater. But I couldn't tell for sure."

"It's gone now," Simon said. "Vanquished by yon gallant hound."

He glanced down at his bare legs, whipped the quilt off his bed, and hastily wrapped it around himself.

"Return to your room without fear, my lady,"

he said in a dignified voice. "I shall stay awake and keep watch until daybreak."

"Thank you, Mr. Nash," Miss Mumsley said, and hurried away, closing the door behind her.

Alex crawled slowly back into his bed. From his pillow, he could see Simon sitting beside the window, squinting fiercely into the night, a loose brick clutched in one hand. He thought for a moment about what Jonathan Periwinkle had said. Something about good intentions. About nice things that people meant to say but never did.

"Simon," he said suddenly.

"Yes, lad?" Simon said, without turning around.

Alex almost stopped himself, feeling silly, but he went ahead anyway.

"I'm awfully glad you're here. You and Tetley and Miss Mumsley. I'm glad we're together. And I'm really grateful for everything you've done."

Simon got to his feet, gathered his quilt about him, and made Alex a deep bow.

"Believe me, Alexander, I am deeply in your debt," he said.

CHAPTER 13

In the Crystal Forest

In which Miss Mumsley
makes a heartfelt discovery

That must be the Crystal Forest," Miss Mumsley said.

"By Saint Norbert's nightcap," Simon said in an awed voice, "it is a faerie land."

"It's exquisite," Miss Mumsley said. "It looks like a forest of diamonds."

They were in a strange silent forest of glass. The trees rose high all around them, translucent as icicles, twigs and branches flashing with rainbow points of light.

"Glass is silly for trees," Tetley said.

The others ignored him.

They tiptoed softly forward, staring up at the glittering foliage. The trees, Alex saw, looking closer, were really tall crystalline formations, like towers of faceted rock candy. From the tips of the branches sprouted flat silvery shapes that seemed to be clusters of tiny geometric leaves. When a breeze ruffled the crystalline branches, the leaves tinkled like silver bells. It was like walking inside a wind chime. Tetley, pattering rapidly forward while looking straight up, thumped heavily into a glassy tree trunk and set off a wild jangle of ringing leaves.

"Why, look," Miss Mumsley said. "Some of them are decorated."

The tree at which she pointed was covered with hundreds of dangling paper stars hung with twists of silver ribbon.

"It's like the Japanese Star Festival," Alex said. "I learned about it at school. People celebrate it by writing wishes on strips of paper and tying them to trees."

"They open," Simon said. "Like wee books."

He opened the nearest star to reveal silver printing inside.

"'I wish I had a pony,'" Alex read.

"Try another," Miss Mumsley said.

"I wish that I were ever wise
Or wore such beauteous disguise
As to seem perfect in your eyes," Simon read, and then turned pink.

"A beautiful sentiment, Mr. Nash," Miss Mumsley said in a soft voice.

"This one isn't," Alex said. "Listen. 'I wish my little brother would disappear.'"

They circled the tree, opening the paper stars, reading the printed wishes, and calling them out to each other.

"'I wish that I, Raymond of the Marl, son of John, Duke of Wolversham, should defeat Geoffrey the Misbegotten in battle.'"

"'I wish that I could whistle.'"

"'I wish that my governess would turn into a lump of yellow soap.'"

"I know what these are," Alex said suddenly. "These are unfulfilled wishes. The wishes that people made that never came true."

"Oh," Miss Mumsley cried. "This one is terribly sad."

Simon bent over her shoulder to read from the star she was holding.

"'I wish for my true love to come home safe to me,'" he read.

"Maybe he was in a war," Alex ventured. "Or a sailor lost at sea."

Miss Mumsley recovered, blowing her nose.

"Or perhaps *she*," she said crisply, "was a balloonist or a traveler on safari in darkest Africa."

Simon opened his mouth and then quickly closed it. Alex suspected that he had been about to say that darkest Africa was no place for a lady.

"Come, my dear," he said, taking Miss Mumsley by the elbow. "We must be moving on."

But soon they found themselves stopping at another decorated tree.

This one was hung with tiny scrolls tied with bits of gold cord. Simon unrolled one.

"'I promise to bequeath to my sister's second son all the lands south of the Old Barley Field,'" he read, "'and my second-best drinking goblet.'"

Miss Mumsley reached for a scroll.

"'I promise never again to gossip with Sarah Scattergood.'"

"'I promise to be home by eight o'clock.'"

"'I promise until this cruel war is over to abjure the nefarious practice of drinking tea.'"

"Listen to this one," Alex said. "'I promise not to tell about the macaroni.' I wonder what that was all about."

"'I promise before I reach the age of three score and ten to make a pilgrimage to Jerusalem,'" Simon read.

"These must be broken promises," Miss Mumsley said.

"Broken vows!" Simon said in a shocked voice.

"Well, some of them are silly," Alex said. "Like the one about never forgetting old friends at Camp Windlethorpe. That can't be very serious."

"A vow," Simon said solemnly, "is a vow. Though, of course, one can be released from an ill-considered vow under certain circumstances."

"Indeed," Miss Mumsley said in a relieved voice. Alex suspected she was thinking of her promise to the faithless Jeremiah Stone.

"I sees hearts," said Tetley.

They had reached the very edge of the forest. Before them was the tallest tree of all, its branches a lacy froth of sparkling crystal. It was covered with dangling hearts that shone in the Moon's blue light like colored gems. As they grew closer, they saw that all of the colored hearts were broken. Some were just chipped a bit, others were cracked in half, and some were shattered all to pieces and held together with bits of string.

"They has names," Tetley said, pointing. "That one is Oliver, see?"

"I don't think so," Miss Mumsley said. "I don't think these are the names of the hearts. Some of them have notes of explanation. 'My dear son, Lester.' 'My faithful dog, Cato.' I think these are the names that caused the hearts to break."

"'Rose Marie, the cancan dancer'?" Simon read in a startled voice.

"'My gallant horse, Paladin.'"

"'Henry.'"

"'Darling Emily.'"

"'My good ship *Windrider.*'"

"This is so sad," Miss Mumsley said with a little catch in her voice.

"Well, there's one here called 'Pootie,'" Alex said. "That's kind of funny, if you ask me."

"It's not the *name* that's sad, Alex," Miss Mumsley said reprovingly. "It's the *feeling.*"

"I sees a pink one," Tetley said.

"Oh, my goodness," Miss Mumsley said.

The pink heart hung at the very end of a branch just above Alex's head. It was a beautiful pink, the soft pure color of sunrises or dewy rosebuds, but like the others it was broken. A thin jagged crack ran straight across it, and it was printed with the words *Jeremiah Stone, Prospector.*

At the sight of the name, Miss Mumsley gave a scornful sniff.

"Nonsense," she said sharply. "The very idea."

She tucked her parasol firmly under her arm, reached upward, and plucked the heart from its branch. As she did, the heart turned pinker than ever. The name promptly faded from its surface and the crack, with a swift little zippery sound, sealed itself back together.

The heart shimmered pinkly for a moment in Miss Mumsley's hand, and Alex, craning forward, thought for a moment that he saw new letters forming upon it. But afterward he could never be sure, for then there was a burst of pink light and the heart disappeared.

"Oh, my goodness," Miss Mumsley said again, looking taken aback. She put one hand to her chest. "Oh, my goodness."

"My dear Edith—Miss Mumsley," Simon stammered, springing forward. "You must sit down. Are you feeling faint?"

"No," Miss Mumsley said faintly. "No, really, Mr. Nash. I am quite recovered now. Quite recovered," she repeated in a firmer voice.

She smiled up at Simon and placed her fingertips lightly on his offered arm.

"Let us proceed," she said. "The time is growing shorter, and we still must find lost time and a lost way."

CHAPTER 14

Skuld

*In which further explanations
are forthcoming*

Which way now?" asked Alex. "Tetley, do you
know where we are?"

They were standing at a crossroads. One
branch of the little lighted path wandered off to
the right, the other to the left.

"I is thinking," Tetley said.

"Well, while Tetley is thinking," Miss Mumsley
said, "I suggest we sit down. We could all do
with a rest. Especially Zeke, poor boy."

She settled herself on a flat rock, adjusting her bustle and shaking out her rose-colored skirts. Simon took the rock beside her, and Alex sprawled out in a soft drift of moondust. Zeke crawled wearily to his side and put his head in Alex's lap. Alex gently stroked his ears.

Tetley pattered nervously back and forth in the crossroads.

"Right!" he said finally, pointing firmly to the left with his hubcap.

"No, Tetley, that's left," Miss Mumsley said.

Tetley pulled his hubcap back and looked upset.

Then abruptly he turned, trotted rapidly back to the rocks where the others were sitting, and ducked behind Miss Mumsley.

"Somebody is there, they is," he said.

"Where?" Miss Mumsley said. "I don't see anyone, Tetley."

"*There,*" Tetley said, not moving. He had put his hubcap over his head.

Alex sat up.

A shadow was forming over a lumpy boulder on the opposite side of the path. As they watched, it solidified and took on the shape of a woman wrapped in a long gray shawl. Her gray hair hung down over her shoulders in a pair of long thick braids, and she carried a large pair of silver scissors.

"So here you are," she said. "And just as I expected. Lass, lad, and Englishman, rat and ancient hound. Well met, travelers, and how goes the journey?"

"Well, I thank you, madam," Simon answered, getting to his feet and bowing nervously in her direction. "And do I have the honor of addressing one of the Norns?"

The woman cackled mirthlessly, showing yellowed teeth.

"No flies on you, my fine young man; I see it takes an early riser to steal a march on *you*. Aye, my dearie, I am Skuld, she as clips the life threads when they reach their ending, and a good job I make of it."

She clacked the blades of her scissors open and shut, grinning at their horrified expressions.

"I am Death, my dears, but no need to look so pasty pale, for I've no hurt to bring you. Rest for the weary is what my scissors offer, and comfort from pain, and when your time comes, you'll see what a gift I offer. Though that's a good while yet I see, except for yon gray dog-gie there with his head down on his paws. He's tired, laddie, tired, and there's not much spin-ning for him left."

"No!" Alex cried, throwing his arms tightly around Zeke. Zeke whuffled sadly and nuzzled at his ear.

"Just a moment," Miss Mumsley said. "That's no fault of this fine dog. He was attacked. His time was stolen by your . . . eating creatures. I think it only fair that the perpetrator, who called itself the Lozar, be punished, and I *demand* that this dog's time be restored to him in full."

The old woman cackled again, rocking back and forth on her boulder.

"A bold brave-spoken lass you are, my dear, but I've naught to do with those who feed on time."

"But we heard you could help us," Alex put in. "To find lost time. I should look for the Norns, she said. The waitress at the Moondust Café."

"Well, she didn't say we eat time, she didn't," the old woman interrupted. "She's a saucy wench, and not above misleading, if the fit takes her, but outright slander she won't do, and you can't tell me different. But if you'll listen quiet and not be argufying and altercating, I'll tell you what you need to know."

"Please," Miss Mumsley said.

The old woman laid her scissors in her lap.

"There are three of us sisters," she said. "Verdande, who does the spinning, Skuld—that's me, my dears—who does the snipping, and Urd, the youngest of us all, who does the fetching and the carrying and the combing of the wool."

Alex gave a tremendous start.

"Is something the matter, Alex?" Miss Mumsley asked.

"Urd," Alex said. "I'm supposed to beware of Urd. That was what Lulu—the lady in the library—said. She told me about the Blue Moon. She has a sister, Selena . . ."

Tetley, from under his hubcap, gave a frightened squeak.

Skuld clucked her tongue.

"And good advice she gave you, dearie. Luna's sharper than she seems to be and a goddess in her own right, for all that it's Selena calls the tune. Mind what she told you now, for Urd's no one to trifle with, not nowadays."

"Lulu's a *goddess*?" Alex said, while at the same time Simon said, "And pray you, lady, what can you tell us of Urd?"

The old woman shook her head.

"Urd, clever lass that she is, grew restless with the sorting and the scrubbing, so she set out to gain power over time. Time present and time past, now those were taken, so Urd, she set her sights on time that is to be."

"The future," Alex said.

Skuld threw him a look.

"Aye, that's right," she said. "A pair of crystal looking-glasses Urd made herself, so that she could see time future. Fresh and golden, she said it was, and she found herself a way of sucking it up, as if it was juice from a peach. And once she saw that that new time could make her ever young, why, then there was no stopping her, and a pretty pickle she's put us all in."

"But . . . what about the Time Eaters?" Alex asked, confused. "Where do they come in?"

Skuld pursed her lips and shook her head.

"Ah, Urd's Gatherers," she said. "Unnatural things, they are, and should be lying quiet, but Urd, she called them up from earth and air and dead men's bones and set them to do her bidding. Fed on time, they are, to keep them walking, and set to gather more, for now that Urd's had a taste of it, she wants more and ever more. First there was one of them, then two, then a dozen, and then a score or more, hollow-hearted demons every one, and a mistake if you ask me."

"I should think so," said Miss Mumsley.

"Why does she need so many of them?" Alex asked.

Skuld gave a dry chuckle.

"It takes a deal of time, my dear, to make a Norn young. We're old, boy, old; time out of mind we've sat here, spinning and snipping, and one lifetime to us is like a single drop in the ocean."

She leaned forward and dropped her voice to a conspiratorial whisper.

"Urd and her servants have built a machine, a machine that harvests time. I've never seen it myself, but I hear that when it's working, a great shuddery sound it makes, like someone beating on a bass drum. They fill it with stolen time—the extras, the time they don't need to feed themselves—huge heaps of it, days and weeks, months and years, decades, centuries, and whole millennia. And it doesn't do to cross the girl, oh mercy no. Anger Urd and off you go to the machine. It takes the time right out of you, it does, and what's left of you comes back looking like nothing so much as the dry cocoon that's left after the butterfly flies away."

"Hideous," Miss Mumsley said in an appalled voice.

"Somebody is *coming*," Tetley said, sounding tinny and muffled. He still had his hubcap over his head.

"Where?" Alex asked.

"There," Simon said, springing to his feet.

It was a Time Eater.

It was just emerging from a patch of blue

mist, a tall cowled figure, its face shrouded in darkness.

Simon bent and picked up a rock. Miss Mumsley got to her feet, brandishing her parasol like a sword. Zeke gave a feeble growl.

"I am the Murgol," the Time Eater whispered. Its voice sounded like wind in a cave.

"There's another," Miss Mumsley said.

A second Time Eater stepped out from behind a great blue rock and moved slowly toward them from the opposite direction.

"I am the Haddag," it whispered in a voice like skeleton bones.

In the distance, the blue mist was rising, and Alex, peering, thought he could see other dark forms, clustered, drifting slowly toward them.

What can we do now? he thought desperately.

Skuld lifted her scissors, clacked the blades open and shut, and waved them in the air.

"If I were you, my dearies," she cackled, "I would run."

CHAPTER 15

The Meadow of Dreams

*In which Alex and his companions
encounter a Hare*

They ran.

Simon flung his rock in the direction of the
first Time Eater, stooped, and hoisted Zeke into
his arms.

"Go!" he shouted. "All of you! Flee for your
lives! I will cover the retreat!"

Miss Mumsley put the hand clutching her
parasol on her hat and seized Tetley's paw with
the other. They dashed down the path, feet

throwing up clouds of blue dust. Miss Mumsley was a surprisingly good runner, Alex noticed, even hampered as she was by button boots, long skirts, and the pink bustle bobbing up and down behind her. She was dragging a terrified Tetley, whose scrabbling paws barely touched the ground.

They all fled, not daring to look behind them. At last, gasping for breath, they stopped at the foot of a little hill and flung themselves down on the ground. Simon was red-faced and wheezing. Alex had a stitch in his side.

"Do—you—see—them, lad?" Simon panted. "Do—they—yet—follow?"

Alex peered behind them into the misty distance.

"I don't see anything," he said.

"They is all gone," Tetley said, rubbing the paw that Miss Mumsley had pulled. "You is fast."

"A veritable Diana," Simon said. "Or a fleet Atalanta, pursuing the golden apples."

Miss Mumsley turned pink.

"I do bends and stretches each morning,"

she said primly. "And a regimen with Indian clubs. Women are no longer merely decorative, Mr. Nash."

"What is this place?" Alex said. "It looks like a cemetery."

"Good heavens," Miss Mumsley said. "So it does."

The hill behind them was studded with row after row of flat stone slabs stuck upright in the ground.

"They has pictures," Tetley said.

They wandered slowly up the hillside, pausing to study the slabs as they passed. On closer examination, the stones didn't look like tombstones after all, Alex reflected. Instead they looked like flickering television sets. The first slab showed a picture of a plump little boy in blue pajamas. He was flying—soaring through a sky full of puffy white clouds with an ecstatic smile on his face. It looked like tremendous fun. As Alex watched, he executed a graceful swan dive into the very center of a cloud, then plunged downward out of the picture and vanished. He reappeared a moment later from the side, gliding serenely on his stomach.

Alex sighed enviously and moved on to the next slab. This one showed a picture of a portly middle-aged gentleman standing at a bus stop holding a briefcase and a rolled umbrella. He was wearing nothing but a pair of red silk boxer shorts. Every few moments he would glance down at himself with an expression of horror. Alex felt sorry for him, but even so he couldn't keep from giggling.

The next slab was the best yet. It showed a tall stone castle, its pointed turrets hung with rainbow-colored banners and its creamy yellow walls covered with climbing roses so lush and many-petaled that Alex could almost smell them. The castle gateway was crowded with people waving and cheering, and advancing ceremoniously at the head of the crowd were a king and queen, both in velvet robes with jeweled crowns on their heads. Their faces were full of joy and welcome. Before them, at the very end of the lowered drawbridge, was a thin little girl with long brown pigtails, wearing a ragged nightgown, and Alex could tell that all the cheering and welcome was just for her. He gazed at the picture with longing.

Zeke, standing raptly in front of a slab behind Alex, gave an excited bark.

"What is it, boy?" Alex asked. He threaded his way between two slabs to see Zeke's picture. "What are you barking at? There's nothing there."

Zeke barked again, louder, and an orange cat shot across the slab, its ears flat back and its tail puffed up like a bottlebrush. It was followed an instant later by a large spotted dog, moving at a gallop. It was grinning and its floppy ears were flapping wildly behind it. It vanished after the cat. The slab was blank for a moment, and then the cat appeared again, still running, looking just as upset as before, still pursued by the spotted dog.

Zeke barked happily and began to wag his tail.

"Ho!" Simon shouted in an agitated voice. "Over here!"

They hurried toward him, dodging between the crowded rows.

"Look!" Simon said, pointing a trembling finger. "It just appeared before me as I stood! Look!"

Tetley squeaked and put his hubcap over his head.

The slab was filled with roiling clouds of blackness. Then shapes appeared in the crawling darkness. First a tiny terrified face popped up in the lower left-hand corner; then, looming hideously over it, rose a monstrous black creature with fangs and outspread arms. The tiny face cowered before it and squinched its eyes tight shut.

There was a sharp *tonk*ing noise that sounded like someone smacking a pair of coconuts together. The tiny face took on an expression of relief and vanished.

"That's a nightmare," a new voice said.

They turned in unison. Behind them stood an immense blue hare.

It was a very elegant hare. Its fur was glossy sky blue, and it wore a quilted coat in royal-blue brocade, embroidered with a pattern of gold and silver stars. It had a gold earring in one long ear, and it carried a polished wooden mallet.

"I wake them up," the Hare explained. It tonked the mallet demonstratively on the edge of a slab.

"But most of them aren't nightmares," it continued cheerfully, lolloping slowly along the line of slabs. "Most of them are quite nice. They're lost dreams, you know. The dreams that people never finish or that they forget about in the morning."

Alex looked at the rows of slabs with new interest. He had once woken from a dream that he just knew was the most marvelous dream he had ever had. The awful part, though, was that he couldn't remember anything about it. Nothing remained but the warm feeling of golden wonder that it had left behind. Every time he fell asleep, he hoped that he would find that dream again, but he never did.

He hurried to catch up with the Hare.

"Oh, it's sure to be here," the Hare said. "But I can't tell you just where. There are so many of them, you see. And new ones arrive all the time."

It sat up higher on its hind legs to look across the hillside and twitched its nose eagerly.

"I'm wasting my time, some of them tell me," it said. "'You're frittering your life away,' they say, 'looking at dream pictures.' But it doesn't seem like a waste to *me*. What do they think time is *for*, anyway?"

"That's what I've been wondering," Alex said unhappily. The awful hopeless feeling was settling in his chest again.

The Hare gave a scornful sniff.

"It's obvious what time is for," it said crossly. "Time is for doing what you love best. *That's* what time is for, I say. But you'd think, to hear *them* jabber, that there was nothing in life but carrots. Root crops and leafy greens, that's all they seem to think about. Time is more than turnips, I tell them, but do they listen?"

It shook its head bitterly, and its long blue ears waggled.

"I think I read a story about you," Alex said. "In a book about China. Some people think that there's a man in the moon, but the Chinese say there's a rabbit."

"That's how it started *out*," the Hare said. "Now there are hundreds of us."

It turned away and began raptly studying a slab that showed a picture of a sunny desert island. There was a bright blue expanse of ocean, a stretch of golden sand, and a grove of palm trees. A little boy in a striped nightshirt was running across the sand wearing a pirate hat and waving a cutlass.

Alex sighed enviously again.

"We're looking for the Pointless Tower," he said. "Do you know which road we should take?"

The Hare pointed, without taking its eyes off the dream picture.

"It's on the next hill," it said vaguely.

Then suddenly it took off at a run, bounding hurriedly across the hillside to bring its mallet down with a *tonk* on a slab in a distant row.

"Thank you," Alex shouted after it.

The Hare didn't answer. It waved absent-mindedly over its shoulder, and the last Alex saw of it, it was lolloping slowly down the rows, pausing here and there to admire the dreams.

CHAPTER 16

The Silver Maze

*In which Zeke takes a turn
for the better*

The pursuit of lost dreams is a futile exercise," Simon said firmly, striding along the path. "One can go on indefinitely, chasing will-o'-the-wisps, without the attainment of one's object." He paused and a worried look flitted across his face. "One can go on and on and on . . ."

Alex tugged at his velvet sleeve.

"Simon," he said warningly.

"There's the tower," Miss Mumsley said.

It was a massive tower of stone topped by an enormous iron arrow like the direction finder on a weathervane. The arrow was spinning ceaselessly in a circle.

"What's all that stuff around it?" Alex asked. "It looks like it's sitting in the middle of a bird's nest."

The tower was surrounded by a thick mass of silver bramble bushes. The bushes rose higher than Simon's head and were covered with vicious needle-sharp thorns. Tetley prodded at them curiously, then yelped, hopped backward, and put his paw in his mouth.

"What dreadful shrubbery," Miss Mumsley said. "We can't possibly get through it. It must have been planted on purpose to keep visitors away."

"Perhaps there's a gap on the other side," Simon said.

They prowled slowly around the perimeter, stopping every now and then to examine the impenetrable mass.

"The mist is rising," Alex said uncomfortably.

A blue mist was creeping toward them across the rocky ground, thickening, gathering, and closing in. First it was ankle deep, and walking through it felt like wading in a puddle of cool cloudy soup. Then it was knee deep, then waist deep, and then it was all about them. Alex could hardly see his hand in front of his face.

"Stay close together now," Miss Mumsley said crisply, taking command. "Hold tight to my parasol, Tetley. Don't wander."

"I is scared," Tetley said in a small voice.

"It will clear in a moment," Miss Mumsley said in a voice of false cheer. "Now don't *crowd,* Tetley."

"Do you smell something?" Alex asked uneasily. It was just a whiff carried on a curl of mist, but it reminded him of moldy cellar holes and spoiled meat. Of the Time Eaters.

Then, frighteningly close on their heels, something began humming. At first the hum was an almost tuneless little chant, repeated over and over; then it suddenly resolved itself into words.

"Man and maiden, beast and bird,
Farmer, wife, and flock and herd,
Father, mother, growing child,
Wise and wicked, weak and wild,
Bad and blameless, foul and fine,
Fair and fearless; all are mine."

Zeke began to growl.

"Faster," Simon said through clenched teeth. They staggered after him through the blinding mist.

"Don't *crowd,* Tetley," Miss Mumsley said again, and then, on a different note, "Tetley? Is that you?"

Then someone yelped and someone shrieked and there was a flurry of thumping sounds. Zeke began to bark frantically.

"Tetley!" Alex shouted. "Miss Mumsley! What's happening?"

Then he was pushed aside as Simon thundered past him, shouting "Edith!" in a panic-stricken voice.

There was more thumping, then a ringing crash, and Simon's voice said, "Ouch!"

"I hit it, I did," said Tetley proudly, from somewhere out of the blueness.

"You hit *me!*" Simon bellowed. *"Edith! Where are you?"*

"I'm right here," Miss Mumsley said, sounding flustered. "I believe it has temporarily retreated. I struck it with my parasol."

"Quickly!" Simon said. "This way!"

They stumbled forward awkwardly, clinging to each other.

"There is smells," Tetley said in a quavering voice. "Behind us."

"Wait," Simon said. "In here."

There was a dark opening in the thorny wall, barely visible through the shifting fog. They ducked into it hastily and stood huddled together, not daring to move. The dank dead smell grew stronger and more piercing. From just outside the wall of silver bushes came the soft shuffle of feet. The Time Eater was less than an arm's reach away.

They could hear it prodding at the thorny tangle. Then, with a muffled cry, it pulled back. It hesitated for a moment, pacing uncertainly back and forth, searching vainly for an entranceway. Then its footsteps moved slowly away.

"At least the creature is not invincible," Simon muttered. "It can be jabbed, just like any other man."

"Where are we?" Miss Mumsley asked. "Could this be the path to the tower?"

They were in a narrow tunnel cut through the thorns. They picked their way cautiously through it single file, making themselves as small as possible to avoid being stabbed. The tunnel twisted and turned, bending first right, then left, and then right again, then bending back upon itself and heading off in the opposite direction.

"Good heavens!" Miss Mumsley exclaimed. "Wherever are we going?"

"It is a maze, my dear," Simon explained in a superior tone of voice. "The secret to finding one's way through it is to follow the right-hand wall, as we are doing. Invariably one emerges."

On his last words, they turned a sharp corner and found themselves in a dead end.

There was a moment of accusing silence.

Then Simon said, "Or perhaps it was the left-hand wall" in much less superior tones, and Tetley stepped backward into the bushes by mistake and screeched.

They retraced their steps and then set off in a different direction, this time winding up in another dead end. They repeated this process several times, becoming crosser by the minute. Alex began to feel dizzy. It seemed as if they had been in the maze for hours, going around in endless circles. Finally, as they were debating a left-hand turn that Alex just knew that they had tried only moments before, Zeke seized him by the pant leg and began to tug weakly, setting up a determined whine.

"He wants us to go that way," Alex said. "See? I told you. We already went left. He's a really smart dog. I think we should do what he says."

"I am willing," Simon said resignedly. "Naught else seems to work."

"*I* have every confidence in Zeke," Miss Mumsley said.

Zeke limped slowly through the silver maze, turning back and forth and back again, leading them down side passages and through confusing little roundabouts. He looked even older now, Alex saw with anguish. He was thinner and grayer; his eyes were dim and sunken, and when he breathed, he wheezed. Still, no matter how tired he was, he refused to give up. He made one last turn to the right and gave an exhausted woof of triumph. They were in front of a wooden door.

"By Saint Edward's eggcup," Simon said reverently, "the gallant hound has done it!"

"He has indeed," Miss Mumsley said. She bent down to stroke Zeke's drooping ear.

"After all that," she continued briskly, "we might as well go in."

CHAPTER 17

The Pointless Tower

*In which a mathematical problem
is satisfactorily solved*

They were in a round stone room, lit by sputtering candles in wall sconces. There were wooden benches edging the walls and scattered about the floor. All of them were filled with people.

There was a trio of explorers in khaki shorts and pith helmets arguing over a map—they were holding it, Alex noticed, upside down—and a pair of aviators in zippered flight suits and leather caps and a sea captain with a wooden leg. The captain was slumped in a corner with a spyglass tucked under one arm and seemed to be asleep.

A cluster of people in colonial garb was camped in the center of the floor next to a mountain man in fringed buckskin and a Spanish conquistador. A red-bearded Viking in a horned helmet shared a bench with an elderly gentleman in a striped dressing gown and a pair of pink-cheeked children holding a basket.

One of the explorers detached himself from the group around the map and came toward them.

"Welcome to the Pointless Tower," he said. "My mates call me Reggie. Sit down and make yourselves comfortable." He waved a hand in the direction of the overcrowded benches. "Somewhere," he added helplessly. "We're a bit full just now."

"Precisely what is this place?" Miss Mumsley asked.

"It's the meeting place for those who have lost their way," Reggie explained. "Complicated things, maps," he added defensively. "With all those little lines and arrows and squiggles and whatzits . . ."

"Indeed," Miss Mumsley said.

"And who, my good sir, might be all these misplaced folk?" Simon asked.

Reggie lowered his voice.

"Those two next to my mates"—he nodded toward the aviators—"lost their landing strip after fooling about in the Bermuda Triangle, and the chap with the fringes"—he pointed at the mountain man—"has lost the Cumberland Gap. The kiddies with the basket—they've lost their way home, due to a misunderstanding with a stepmother and some silly business with dropped bread crumbs. The big bearded bloke with the horns—he's lost Iceland, his ship, and his temper; and all the folk there in the middle with the bundles, they've lost a whole colony, lock, stock, and barrel. Some island with an *R*."

"What about the sea captain?" Alex said.

"He's lost a whale," Reggie said. "A white one. Somewhere in the Atlantic Ocean. Mean as a snake to hear him tell about it, though if I were you, I wouldn't ask. And the Spaniard, he's lost seven cities of gold. Up there"—he pointed toward the eaves—"we've got homing pigeons who couldn't find their way back to their roosts, and under the staircase there's a bunch of rats who couldn't find their way out of laboratory mazes. And the fellow in the bathrobe, *he* took a wrong turn down a corridor and lost his hotel room."

"Goodness," Miss Mumsley said.

"Well, I'd best be getting back," Reggie said. "Heading for Alice Springs, we are, and that map is nothing but a heap of trouble." He looked appealingly at Alex. "Latitude, now, that runs sideways, doesn't it?"

Before Alex could answer, Reggie's companions began to shout at each other and tug at opposite sides of the map, which tore in two.

"Never mind, then," Reggie said. He waved back over his shoulder. "Ta-ta for now."

"Goodness," Miss Mumsley said again.

"There is writing on the walls," Tetley said.

The walls were covered with graffiti, scratched

with pocketknives, scribbled with pencils, or printed in ballpoint pen.

"Why, Dr. Livingstone was here," Miss Mumsley said. "It says 'Dr. David Livingstone, Somewhere in Africa, 1869.'"

"Here's the entire crew of a ship called the *Flying Dutchman*," Alex said. "A lot of them sign their name with *X*s."

"'Sir John de Mandeville, Knight, en route to the fabled land of Prester John.'"

"'Captain Henry Hudson, shamefully betrayed by my crew and set adrift somewhere in the Bay that bears my name.'"

"'Robinson Crusoe.'"

"'Amelia Earhart.'"

"'Stairs.'"

"What?" Alex said.

"Stairs," Tetley repeated. "See? Stairs."

There was a doorway in a little alcove with a sign over it that read STAIRS.

"See?" Tetley said again smugly.

Simon opened the door—it made an unhappy rasping noise—and peered inside.

"Stairs," he said. "Going upward."

"Well, let's climb them," Miss Mumsley said. "There may be something useful at the top. Certainly no one seems to know much down here."

The stairs ended in a strange little room at the very top of the stone tower. It was completely surrounded by round windows like portholes, and there was a metal pole in the middle of the floor connected to the spinning directional arrow on the tower roof. They could hear the creaking sound that the arrow made as it turned. It sounded like a ship under full sail.

At a desk in the middle of the floor sat a man who looked like a college professor, busily scribbling in a large leather-bound ledger. He glanced up as they entered and peered at them over the tops of his spectacles.

"Take a seat right over there," he said impatiently, pointing at a row of chairs along the wall. "I'll be with you in just a moment."

He scribbled one last phrase, ending in a flourish, and closed the book.

"I trust you have an appointment?"

"No," Miss Mumsley said. "No, I'm afraid we don't. To tell the truth, we didn't expect to find anyone up here. We were merely exploring."

"No matter," the professor said, waving his pen in the air. "No matter. Missed appointments are one of our specialties. We also deal in forgotten points of order, mislaid points of argument, and, of course"—he waved a hand toward a large glass jar at the side of the desk— *"these."*

"What's that?" Alex asked. "Pepper?"

"Oh, no, no," the professor said fussily, tapping the jar with his pen. "Oh, no, no. Though there are certain inconvenient similarities. These, young man, are misplaced decimal points. And much in demand they are. Why, lose one of these, and ten becomes ten thousand, two becomes two million, or five hundred turns into the tiniest fraction of a fraction of a—"

He stopped abruptly.

"They move around, you see," he said. "It makes it hard to pin them down."

He lifted the lid from the jar and shoved it toward them invitingly.

"Would you like a closer look?"

Simon was leaning forward in his chair with a dazed look on his face. He muttered something under his breath. It sounded like "on and on and on." Alex poked him sharply in the ribs.

"Go ahead," he whispered.

Simon got up, gathering his velvet robe about him, approached the desk, and—with Alex and Tetley crowding curiously at his elbows—peered into the jar. It was filled with thousands and thousands of tiny black specks that looked just like black pepper. Simon poked an inquisitive finger into the jar and stirred the contents experimentally. For a moment nothing happened.

Then Tetley's whiskers began to twitch, he snuffled helplessly, pawed the air, and gave a tremendous sneeze, dropping his hubcap with a jangling crash.

Alex felt his own nose begin to tickle.

He staggered back from the jar, trying to muffle the impending explosion. It was impossible.

He burst out with a reverberating *Ah-choo!* that made his ears ring and his eyes water.

"Ah . . ." Simon said.

"Put your finger under your nose, Mr. Nash," Miss Mumsley suggested hurriedly.

"Ah . . ." Simon said again. He was turning red in the face.

"Simon?" Alex said nervously.

"Ah . . . ah . . . AH . . . AH-CHOO!"

The professor sprang forward and hastily clapped the lid back on the jar.

"They're quite potent," he said. "Surprisingly so, considering their size. Are you feeling better now?"

Simon, looking astounded, was mopping his face with a large linen handkerchief.

"By Saint Perpetua's pudding basin," Simon said. "By Saint Ursula's undergarments. By Saint Martin's mustard jar. By . . ."

He paused for so long that Alex wondered if he had run out of saints. Then he turned to the professor.

"Might I trouble you, good sir, for a parchment and a quill?"

The professor found him a yellow legal pad and a pencil.

"Repeating fractions," Simon muttered, writing

rapidly. He seemed to like pencils. "Arithmetical series. Decimal points." His lips were turned up in a satisfied smile.

"I have discovered," he announced in triumphant tones, "a new mathematical principle. I am calling it 'infinity.' It goes on and on and on and . . ." He stopped, feeling their worried eyes upon him.

"And on," he finished firmly.

"Do I take it, Simon dear," Miss Mumsley inquired, "that you have found your lost way?"

There were congratulations all around, and the professor, warming to a fellow academic with an appreciation for decimal points, produced a large box of cream biscuits and a decanter of fine old brandy from a bottom drawer of his desk and passed plates and glasses. For Alex, he found a bottle of raspberry ginger ale. They all toasted Simon (several times), and Tetley got the hiccups again.

When the impromptu celebration was over, Alex realized that he was feeling very alone.

"So you're both done," he said, looking from Simon to Miss Mumsley and back again. "You've both found what you were looking for. Now you'll be able to go home."

"Not yet, lad," Simon said heartily, clapping him on the shoulder. "There's still some time left to us. We wouldn't leave you here, with *your* task yet unfinished, and there's Zeke to think of too. Would we, Edith? Tetley?"

Tetley hiccupped and shook his hubcap.

"Of course not," Miss Mumsley said. "Certainly not. One for all and all for one, as dear Mr. Dumas so aptly put it. We're all in this together. Now it's simply a matter of discovering what to do next."

"Could you help us?" Alex asked the professor. "I'm trying to find lost time. Do you know where I'm supposed to go?"

In answer, the professor pointed upward. The creaking sound had ceased.

Atop the Pointless Tower, the great spinning iron arrow had come to a stop.

CHAPTER 18

An Unpleasant Cavern

*In which there are confusions
and disagreements*

That way," Alex said firmly. "That's the way the arrow pointed. Toward that mountain."

"A pretty distance," Simon said, squinting into the mist.

Alex didn't see what was pretty about it.

"We'll never make it," he said dismally. "It's too far. Three days at most, that's what Lulu said. Our time must be nearly up."

"Well it's not up yet," Miss Mumsley said

briskly, hoisting her parasol. "And we can't succeed unless we try. Perhaps," she added hopefully, "it's not as far as it looks."

"Perhaps," she added after another minute, "we should all walk faster."

"Then Zeke won't be able to keep up," Alex said miserably.

Zeke seemed to grow older and weaker by the minute. It was clear that he had almost reached the limit of his endurance. He whimpered, ears drooping sadly, and nudged Alex's hand.

It soon became clear that they were not going to get far. The blue night was falling and a chilly wind had risen, which threw stinging dust into their eyes. The sky darkened to royal blue, then to indigo, and then to a deep inky blue-black. The air grew colder. In spite of himself, Alex began to think longingly of the rickety beds at the Inn of Abandoned Plans.

"Ho! Here, ahead!"

It was Simon, shouting to be heard above the wind. They hurried toward him, stumbling over the uneven ground. Simon was standing at the dark entrance to what appeared to be a cave.

"Shelter for the night," he explained.

"Why, how clever of you, Mr. Nash," Miss Mumsley said.

Alex eyed the cave with misgiving. It looked awfully dark. Anything could be in there, he thought uneasily. Bears. Snakes. Goblins. But Simon and Miss Mumsley had already stepped inside. Alex and Zeke followed, closely trailed by Tetley, who had put his hubcap over his head.

The interior of the cave, however, was a pleasant surprise. It was dimly lit by a pale-blue fluorescent light and was crowded with large flat rocks covered with thick spongy blue moss. Miss Mumsley gave the moss an experimental pat.

"Quite warm and dry," she said. "These should make excellent beds."

She sat down on the nearest rock, removed her hat with the painted cherries, and then stretched out cautiously on her side, pillowing her head on her parasol.

"Extremely comfortable," she said.

Alex climbed onto a rock beside her. It *was* comfortable. The moss was soft and springy, like foam rubber, and smelled vaguely of peppermint. He could feel himself sinking into it as he lay down. Zeke scrambled up beside him and curled up at his feet. There were some thumps from a far corner as Simon settled himself on a rock and pulled off his boots. Tetley was already asleep, lying on his back with his mouth open, his hubcap clutched in his paws. Alex realized that he was terribly tired. It did make sense to rest for a bit. They'd make better progress in the morning. Almost before he finished his thought, he fell asleep.

He was awakened by voices. At first he thought it was his mother calling him. He had been so soundly asleep that he had forgotten where he was. He thought he was in his own bed at home and he had overslept again and was about to miss the school bus. Then he realized that it wasn't his mother's voice at all. It was a voice he'd never heard before and it was absolutely furious.

"GET YOUR BIG FLAT FEET OFF MY ARTI-CHOKES!" the voice bellowed angrily, right into Alex's ear. It sounded as if it belonged to an outraged elderly man.

Alex opened his eyes with a start.

"SHUT UP!" another voice shouted shrilly, from somewhere near the ceiling. "SHUT UP! SHUT UP! SHUT UP!" It sounded a bit like Alex's four-year-old cousin, Charles, throwing a tantrum.

"How *dare* you, Mr. Billingsgate!" shrieked a female voice. "Unhand me, sir!"

"STOP PLAYING THOSE BLASTED BAG-PIPES!"

"DROP THAT SLIPPER, YOU WRETCHED DOG!"

Zeke lifted his head and gave an upset woof.

Alex rubbed his eyes and struggled to sit up.

"YOU DIRTY RAT!" someone roared behind him. Alex whirled around but there was no one there. Tetley, whose whiskers had gone crooked in the night, sat up and gave a protesting squeak.

Simon, looking bleary-eyed and rumpled, rolled over and began groping for his boots.

"What on earth is going on?" Miss Mumsley said.

"YOU'VE SPILLED IT AGAIN, YOU FLAMING IDIOT!" someone screeched.

Alex suddenly realized that he felt monumentally cross.

"How am I supposed to know?" he snapped.

"There's no need to be rude, young man!" Miss Mumsley snapped back.

"Must there be these continual unseemly insults?" demanded Simon grumpily. He stood up, jerking at his crumpled velvet robe, and stamped his feet.

"SHUT UP!" the ceiling voice shouted.

"What possessed you to choose this perfectly dreadful cave?" Miss Mumsley said, glaring angrily at Simon.

"And perhaps *you* had had a better proposal?" Simon said coldly, glaring back.

"GIVE ME BACK MY PRETZELS!" someone shrieked behind him.

Zeke began to growl.

"Dogs is mean," Tetley muttered into his hubcap.

Alex scrambled off his rock.

"Come on, everybody," he said. "Something's wrong. We've got to get out of here!"

"OUT!" a voice screamed from somewhere near Alex's ankles. "OUT! OUT! OUT! GET OFF MY DOORSTEP, STANLEY DOOLITTLE, AND NEVER SHOW YOUR FACE HERE AGAIN!"

Alex grabbed Tetley's paw and headed hastily for the cave entrance, with Zeke limping at his heels. Miss Mumsley stalked angrily after them, putting on her hat, looking as if she had just taken a bite of a very sour pickle. Simon, with a face like thunder, brought up the rear. They emerged into the bluish light of early morning and stood shaking their heads and staring at each other. A horrified look crept across Miss Mumsley's face.

"I can't think what came over me," she said in a shamed voice.

"Perhaps some dark bewitchment," Simon said.

He removed his velvet cap.

"I beg all of you to accept my deepest apologies," he said.

"Dogs is nice," Tetley was explaining hurriedly into his hubcap. "Dogs is very, very nice."

"That's what the matter is," Alex said suddenly. "We must have missed it last night in the dark. Look!"

He pointed at a spot above their heads.

A sign was wedged between the rocks high over the cave entrance. BEWARE! it said. CAVERN OF LOST TEMPERS. ENTER AT YOUR OWN RISK!

"They must have sort of infected us while we were asleep," Alex said. "That's why we all woke up so cross."

"Of course," Miss Mumsley said, nodding.

"A veritable plague of anger," Simon said. "Waiting for the unwary traveler."

"Thank heavens you saw what was happening," Miss Mumsley said to Alex. "Why, everyone knows that once tempers are lost, common sense goes out the door. We might just have sat there squabbling for goodness knows how long."

Alex thought worriedly about all the times

he'd lost his temper. Was his voice in there somewhere, yelling at people to shut up? It was an uncomfortable thought. He resolved to be more careful in the future.

"We'd best be off," Simon said.

CHAPTER 19

A Visit to the Rats

*In which Alex and his companions find
an unexpected means of transport*

They had walked a mile or more when, from
somewhere just ahead, there came an earsplitting explosion.

Everyone jumped.

"What was *that*?" Alex said.

"That," Tetley said proudly, "is *rats*."

"That," Miss Mumsley said disapprovingly a
moment later, "is *trash*."

They had come to an enormous junkyard.

Alex had never seen so much junk in his life. There were towering piles of pipes and wheels and old tin cans, bulging bins of nails and screws and gears, heaps of decrepit-looking machines, and—scattered about like robotic tumbleweed—curling rolls of ragged sheet metal and tangled bales of wire.

The yard was full of Moon Rats. There were rats everywhere, clambering over the piles of debris, flinging things about, banging on things, falling over each other, and squabbling at the tops of their voices. Groups of rats were cobbling pieces of junk into enormous devices that didn't seem to do much of anything—there was a large insectile contraption that appeared to be covered with pinwheels—and one rat, wearing sunglasses and a very large baseball cap, was doing something to a wheel-less bicycle with a sputtering blowtorch. Every once in a while, from one or another of the jumbled piles, there was a loud explosion, followed by a fountain of colored sparks.

"Those is fireworks," Tetley said. "All the ones that doesn't explode comes here."

There was a thunderous bang from a pile to their right, followed by a piercing squeal and a puff of green smoke.

"Sometimes they explodes *later*," Tetley said.

There was a confusion of shrieks and outcries from a nearby gang of rats who had been tugging at a torn canvas covering something lumpy and large.

"It's Tetley! And Alex!"

"They got here, they did!"

"I said so all along. He'll be fine, I said, what with Tetley to help him and all. And here they are, see?"

"Ouch! Stop shoving!"

"You shoved first!"

"Did not!"

"Did too!"

"Pooptail!"

"Stinkhead!"

Two of the rats began to scuffle.

It was Scrubber and the crew from the spaceship.

"Hi," Alex said. "It's nice to see you all again." He quickly introduced Simon and Miss

Mumsley. "This is Scrubber," he said. "And Opie and Perline and Elveeta." He paused. The crew seemed to have multiplied.

"Aren't there more of you?" he asked.

Scrubber waved an expansive paw. "We're on a new project now," he said importantly, "and we've had to bring in extras. Those two there"—he pointed at the scufflers—"are Pimento and Diesel. This here is Figbar"—a slightly cross-eyed rat wearing mismatched galoshes and a purple bandanna—"and that one there, with the hammer, is Fritter."

He moved closer to Alex and spoke confidentially.

"Plenty of places for you, too, if you'd like to lend a hand. And your friends and all."

"Thanks," Alex said, "but I don't think so right now. We're headed over there—to the mountain. We shouldn't even stay to talk now. We have to get moving. I don't have much time left."

"We could help them, we could, boss." It was Perline, sounding excited.

"They could take the new project, like."

"Can't. The new project won't go yet."

"Will too."

"Will not."

"Smellears."

"Excuse me," Miss Mumsley said loudly. "Just what is this new project?"

"We'll show you, see?" Scrubber said.

Pushing, squealing, and stepping on each other, the rats dashed toward the mysterious lump under the canvas and started to tug the cover away. First, rats to the right and left of the lump tugged in opposite directions, which caused the canvas to split in the middle and led to more squabbling. Then they all changed sides and made the same mistake again. Finally, after a lot of frantic reshuffling, they all managed to tug in the same direction at the same time. The cover slid off, and the lump beneath was gloriously revealed.

It was an airplane.

Alex goggled at it.

"Good heavens," Miss Mumsley said.

"By Saint Sylvester's stocking tops," Simon said, "what manner of contrivance is this?"

The rats and Alex simultaneously explained.

Then—while the rats bickered among themselves, to a chorus of "You interrupted, you did!" and "Shut up!" and "Me first!"—Alex explained again. When Simon and Miss Mumsley finally understood that the new machine was not an odd sort of wagon but was designed to fly high in the air like a bird, both assumed identical expressions of deepest apprehension.

"It can't possibly be safe," Miss Mumsley said. "Just look at it."

Alex had to admit that they had a point. The airplane looked like it was falling apart. It had been pieced together from a wild assortment of odds and ends. One wing was larger than the other, and both were covered with flattened tomato soup cans. The propeller looked suspiciously like an old electric fan, and the instrument panel consisted of a row of doorknobs, a manual typewriter keyboard, and a lot of little metal tubes held in place by rubber bands.

"Does it really fly?" he asked.

"Of course it flies," said Scrubber in an offended voice. "And it's safe too. See? There is seat belts."

"This lever makes it go up and down, see?"

"And there is foot pedals for landing."

"And a steering wheel, see?"

It couldn't be worse than the spaceship, Alex reflected.

"I *have* to go," he said to his companions. "At least Zeke and I have to go. Our time is running out. It's our only chance."

"Not alone," Simon said. He gulped and threw an anxious look at the airplane. "We'll see this adventure through to the end together. One for all and all for one. But . . . canst fly this air carriage, lad?"

"I flies it, see?" Tetley said. He lowered his aviator goggles importantly. "I knows how."

There was a short pause.

"I'm sure we'll be perfectly fine," Miss Mumsley said in a not-quite-convincing voice.

After a pause for a brief meal of cheese, during which Simon talked gloomily of last suppers, they climbed awkwardly into the airplane. Miss Mumsley, Simon, and Alex settled themselves in a row of cramped plastic chairs fastened to the floor with duct tape. Zeke crouched exhaustedly on the floor, and Tetley, bombarded from all sides with contradictory instructions from Scrubber and crew, sat in the pilot's chair.

"Ready for takeoff, you is!" someone shouted.

Alex's stomach gave a nervous leap.

"Flaps down!"

"No, up!"

"Use that knob, see!"

At the front of the airplane, Fritter was pounding vigorously on the propeller with a hammer.

Alex turned to see how the other passengers were doing. Miss Mumsley had her eyes squeezed tight shut. Beside her, Simon looked pale.

"Clear the runway!"

Frantic rats dashed in front of them, kicking cracked buckets and broken bicycles out of the way.

"Now!"

Alex took a deep breath while Tetley, using both paws, pulled up on the lever.

The airplane lumbered forward, bucked and shuddered, and hurled itself, lurching and hiccupping, into the air.

CHAPTER 20

The Third Sister

*In which there is a fateful but
unfortunate meeting*

The airplane flight was quite fun. In spite of all
the worries and fears about what was facing him
ahead, Alex found that he was enjoying himself.
Miss Mumsley had managed to open her eyes,
and Simon had entered into the spirit of the
thing and was leaning over the plane's side to
get the full effect of the view from the air.

As they neared the mountain, Alex began
searching worriedly for a place to land. At first,

nothing seemed quite right. There was a plateau, but it was dotted erratically with stunted silvery trees and solid-looking blue boulders. There was a clear patch ahead, though, that looked like it would do, if Tetley could manage to maneuver the plane into it. He shouted and pointed. Tetley nodded enthusiastically and yanked with both paws on the lever. The plane dropped sharply toward the ground. Alex felt as if the bottom had dropped out of his stomach.

He glanced rapidly over his shoulder and saw that Miss Mumsley had closed her eyes again. Simon had turned an unhealthy shade of green.

Tetley tramped down hard on the pedals. The plane gave a tremendous hiccup and spat out a cloud of black smoke. The propeller began to make a loud ratchety noise that reminded Alex of someone dragging a stick along a picket fence. Then it seesawed indecisively, dipped its nose, and barreled furiously toward the plateau.

"Hang on!" Alex shouted.

Tetley tugged wildly at the steering wheel. Zeke began to howl. The plane bounced, jounced, and abruptly hit the ground, where it skidded hysterically, snapping off several of the silvery trees, spun in a circle, and came to a stop. After a moment, a sound like a stack of soup cans falling over came from inside the engine and the propeller stopped spinning.

"We is down," Tetley said brightly.

"Merciful heavens," Miss Mumsley said, drawing a long breath.

They climbed slowly out of the airplane, all feeling rather wobbly in the knees.

"Well done, brave rat," Simon said weakly. He was beginning to get his normal color back.

Zeke gave a relieved woof.

Miss Mumsley straightened her hat and tucked her parasol firmly under her arm.

"What next?" she said.

"It seems likely," Simon said, pointing, "that we go there."

At the far end of the plateau, balanced at the edge of a plunging precipice, stood a castle. Or rather a fortress. The building was a huge windowless block of black stone, fronted with a long row of stone steps and a massive iron-barred door. It looked ugly and threatening. It squatted heavily on its cliff top like a monstrous stone toad.

They walked toward it reluctantly, Zeke limping painfully beside them. Alex could hardly bear to watch him.

As they drew closer to the castle, they saw that someone was sitting on the stone steps. She stood up as they approached. Alex stared. This wasn't at all what he had expected. A Time Eater, perhaps, or another of those strange old women—but this was a young girl, not much older than he was himself, with long golden curls cascading down the middle of her back. She wore a filmy blue dress the color of the Moon's strange mist and a pair of tiny blue slippers with jeweled ankle straps.

She raised a slender hand in greeting. When she spoke, her voice sounded like silver bells.

"Greetings, strangers, and welcome," she said.

"But what brings you here on such a long journey, to my castle at the very world's end? For from here you can go no farther; neither can you easily return."

She smiled at them with little pink lips, and Alex found that he didn't like her at all. It was just a feeling, but he knew he couldn't be wrong. No matter how sweetly she smiled, this girl wasn't friendly.

"Who are you?" he asked bluntly.

"Why, you know who I am, my lovely boy," the girl said, "fresh from meeting my sisters as you are, though I've not had a chance yet to tell my side of the story, and a fine tale I shall make of it, though you may not like the ending."

She turned to Simon, who was staring with his mouth open, and gave a tinkling little laugh. "Did you not guess my name, my clever scholar? Or you, my lissome lady?"

Alex felt a startled jolt of recognition.

"I know who you are," he said. "You're the youngest Norn. The third sister."

The girl held out her filmy skirts and danced lightly on her toes.

"That I am, my sweeting, the youngest and cleverest of them all, and my name is Urd."

"Clever is as clever does," Miss Mumsley said tartly.

The girl made a pouty little face.

"So *they* said," she answered. "And there *they* sit with their spinning and snipping, so old the two of them, with their wrinkles and their gray hairs and their knobby fingers." Her voice grew mocking. "It was 'Take this, Urd' and 'Fetch that, Urd' and 'Mend the baskets' and 'Wash the wool,' but now we'll see who calls the tune."

She twirled in a circle, making her filmy skirts swirl around her.

"Soon, if they want time for their spindle and their scissors, they'll have to come to me, and not a driblet will they get, not even if they ask ever so nicely."

"*I'm* looking for lost time," Alex said. "That's why I'm here. There's a watch that belongs to me. Do you know if it's here?"

Urd gave a trilling little laugh.

"I can see time," she said slyly. "I can find it and I can take it, but I never, ever give it back."

A stubborn look washed over her pretty face. "Finders keepers," she said.

"Selfish, greedy little beast," Miss Mumsley muttered.

Urd slipped a hand into a pocket of her gown and pulled out a pair of strange-looking spectacles. The frames were silver, and the lenses were thick multifaceted bubbles of glass, like the prisms on chandeliers. When she set them on her slender nose, they gave her the goggly look of a surprised grasshopper. Where light hit the glass lenses, it glittered in reflected rainbow colors.

"I can see time clear as clear," the girl giggled. "Golden all about you, sugar-sweet, and ripe for the picking, if only you knew how. *I* know how, I do, but I'm not telling."

"Those must be the crystal looking-glasses," Simon murmured. "The ones the aged scissor lady spoke of."

"It's theft, you know," Miss Mumsley said sternly. "Snatching people's time away without so much as a by-your-leave. Look what your minions have done to Zeke here."

Alex suddenly had a horrid thought.

"How long have you been doing this?" he demanded. He turned from Simon to Miss Mumsley and back again. "Don't you see what it means? All the people who die before their time—it's because she's taken it. She's killing people. I'll bet she's been doing it for ages."

Urd had taken off her glittering glasses. Now she looked sullen.

"It's fair," she said sulkily. "They don't even know they have it. Why should they care? And I need time. I need it. You can't take it away from me. You can't stop me. You're not clever enough."

She shook her golden curls and leaned forward conspiratorially.

"I can take your time too, you know," she whispered. "If I want to."

As if on cue, the great door behind her swung open. Zeke growled feebly and Tetley gave a squeak of dismay. A line of cowled figures stood there. Time Eaters.

"Take them to the dungeon!" Urd cried, twirling gleefully on her toes.

The Time Eaters, moving as one, stepped forward. Alex took a frantic look behind him at the sheer drop of the stony cliffs. There was no place to run.

Urd began to laugh.

CHAPTER 21

Down in the Dungeon

*In which Tetley has
an unlikely key*

The dungeon of Urd's castle was cold, dank, and dark. The only light was a dim blue murk, filtering fitfully in from a narrow slit in the wall high above them. They were locked in the largest of the dungeon's cells, imprisoned behind a barred door that fastened with an intimidating padlock the size of a dinner plate.

Alex sat miserably on the stone floor, one arm around Zeke, whose head rested equally miserably on Alex's knees. Simon and Miss Mumsley sat dejectedly side by side on a moldy bale of straw. Tetley huddled in a corner, muttering mournfully into his hubcap. Life had never looked bleaker.

The Blue Moon was almost over. They would never get home again. They would all sit here, shivering and hungry, until the Time Eaters came back to drain them of their time, turning them in an instant into withered mummies. Alex thought sadly of his parents. They would never know what had happened to him. He hoped they would forgive him for all the trouble he had caused them. He wished they'd all had more time together. The thought of time brought him up short. He felt awful enough to cry.

Miss Mumsley got abruptly to her feet and began to pace back and forth across the cell.

"We must think of something to do," she said. "We simply cannot all sit here waiting to be . . . *picked* like peas! Perhaps when one of those creatures returns, we could overpower it. Surely all of us, working together, could manage to seize it through the bars."

"What we need," Simon said, angrily rattling the padlock, "is a key."

"I has keys," Tetley said.

He dug in the pocket of his tool belt and produced a confusing mass of keys. He had dozens of all shapes and sizes, threaded onto a length of twine. There were tiny brass keys that looked like they went to someone's diary or jewelry box, medium-sized steel keys that looked like the sort that opened money boxes and lockers, and big fancy bronze keys with lacy metal grips that looked like old-fashioned house keys.

"We'll take it in turns," Miss Mumsley said, "and we'll try them all. You start, Tetley. They're your keys."

They tried key after key, first hopefully, and then becoming more and more discouraged. Nothing worked. They tried the large keys first, since those looked most likely to fit the enormous lock, then the medium-sized keys, and finally, in despair, the small keys, right down to the tiniest key of all, which was no bigger than a paper clip.

"It's no good," Alex said at last. He handed the string of keys back to Tetley. "None of them fits."

"I has one more," Tetley said.

He groped in the pocket of his tool belt and produced one last key. The new key had a plain cylindrical barrel and a double handle shaped like a figure eight. Along one side were engraved the words *Superior Rollerskate Company*.

"That won't work," Alex said disgustedly. "It's an old skate key. It's not for locks."

"It can't hurt to try," Miss Mumsley said.

Tetley pattered over to the enormous padlock, tucking his hubcap firmly underneath his arm. He steadied the lock with one paw and carefully inserted the skate key in the keyhole. Alex held his breath.

Tetley turned the key.

There was a loud click and the lock sprang open.

Alex's mouth fell open. Tetley threw him a smug look.

"Bravo, good rat!" cried Simon.

Miss Mumsley kissed Tetley on the nose.

They stumbled into the dark corridor, where there was a confused moment of people falling over each other and walking into each other and saying "That way!" and "No, this way!" all at the same time. At last they sorted themselves out and headed toward a dim archway in the distance, faintly lit by a flickering torch in a wall bracket.

They never reached it.

"There is smells," Tetley whispered.

Simon, in the lead, stopped dead, extending a warning arm. They were not alone.

A tall hooded figure paced silently past the archway and vanished, apparently down a corridor on the other side. It was followed by another figure, and then another and another in an eerie procession, like marchers in a ghostly parade. Each marcher carried a tall staff and every second or third carried a lantern that emitted a pale-blue light through a series of narrow horizontal slits.

"Time Eaters," Simon whispered.

They stood frozen, hardly daring to breathe. The Time Eaters continued to glide by in stately single file. Another passed the archway and disappeared out of sight. Then another.

And then Tetley hiccupped.

The last Time Eater hesitated and stopped in its tracks. It turned slowly, raising one withered clawlike hand, peering blindly toward them. Alex could just see the bright pinpoints of its eyes. Had it heard Tetley? Could it see them in the dark? *Smell* them?

He stepped cautiously backward, flattening himself against the wall. Then his heart gave a sudden leap. Instead of the rough stone wall, his hands had encountered the smooth wooden panels of a door.

The Time Eater took a step toward them, peering, moving its hooded head back and forth. It seemed puzzled.

Silently Alex swept his fingers over the surface of the closed door. There were metal lumps that felt like nails, and a long metal tongue that felt like part of a hinge. Hurriedly he moved his hand the other way. More nails. And then a fat smooth metal doorknob.

He nudged Miss Mumsley, who was standing next to him, and whispered, barely making a sound.

"There's a door."

The Time Eater took another step and gave a long low hiss.

"I am the Gorzag," it whispered in its hollow ghost-voice.

Miss Mumsley poked Alex with her parasol.

"Open it," she mouthed urgently.

Alex hesitated, grasping the knob. *Anything could be in there,* he thought.

The Time Eater took another tentative step.

"Open it!" Miss Mumsley mouthed again.

"What's going on?" Simon mouthed from over Miss Mumsley's shoulder.

Tetley suddenly buried his face in his paws.

"What's wrong, Tetley?" Alex whispered.

Tetley, still buried, shook his head violently. His ears were twitching. Clearly he was under some terrible stress. He flapped a helpless paw. Then suddenly he gave another tremendous hiccup.

The Time Eater raised its staff high and pounded it thunderously on the floor.

"I AM THE GORZAG! Who walks there?"

Whatever was on the other side of the door,

Alex decided, couldn't possibly be worse than what was about to be right here. He twisted the knob and, with a thrust of his shoulder, shoved the door open. It swung silently on oiled hinges, opening onto a shadowed stone hallway.

The Time Eater was pacing swiftly toward them now. Behind it, in the archway, its fellows were returning, summoned by the pounding of the staff. One of them held its lantern high, throwing striped beams of flickering blue across the walls and floor of the corridor. The strange light made the Time Eaters appear phosphorescent. The dark folds of their robes were streaked with flashes of cold pale blue, their crooked fingers flexed to show glowing curved nails, and their shriveled lips peeled back to reveal glowing teeth.

"Through here!" Alex bellowed.

They darted through the open doorway, and Simon, bringing up the rear, slammed the wooden door in the Gorzag's face. Then Tetley took the Superior Rollerskate key out of his tool-belt pocket, inserted it in the keyhole, and turned it. The lock clicked shut with a satisfying snap. From the other side of the panels came a chorus of angry whispers, and the door shuddered as someone pounded on it furiously with a staff.

"I locked it, I did," Tetley said, and hiccupped.

Miss Mumsley burst into tears.

CHAPTER 22

The Carved Clock

*In which Alex produces a
timely solution to a riddle*

They stood on the stone-flagged floor of the hallway, deciding what to do next. Miss Mumsley, looking embarrassed, was mopping her eyes with her handkerchief. She never cried, she explained to everyone. Never. And certainly not in public. It was a feminine weakness that she utterly despised. It was the stress, she said, and the shocking lack of sleep. Simon put a protective arm about her shoulders, and everyone else tactfully pretended to be interested in the stonework of the walls and ceiling.

When Miss Mumsley had recovered—though still a bit watery and pink about the eyes and nose—they began explore their surroundings. This took little time. The hallway was long, blank, and empty, and it smelled moldy and unused. The only way out was the locked door behind them.

"A veritable oubliette," Simon muttered unhappily.

"It turns a corner up ahead," Miss Mumsley said hopefully, clearing her throat. "Perhaps . . ."

They turned the corner and came face to face with a solid wall against which stood an enormous grandfather clock.

There was a moment of horrified silence.

"Now we does what?" said Tetley.

The clock towered above them. They had to tilt their heads back to look up at its face, which was elaborately painted with gold Roman numerals. On one half of the face, there was a picture of a golden sun with glaring eyes and snarling lips and a lot of curling golden rays that looked like wild hair. On the other was a placid-looking silver moon with its eyes closed.

The case of the clock was covered with carvings of birds and animals and people and strange creatures with human faces but the legs and horns of goats or the clawed feet of eagles or the bodies of horses. There was a glass door behind which an immense brass pendulum swung rhythmically back and forth. Beside the door was a life-size carving of an old man holding a scythe.

"Father Time," Miss Mumsley said.

There were carved letters, inlaid with silver, on the curving blade of the scythe.

" *'Time passes ever,'* " Alex read aloud. " *'Time waits never. / Your Time tend, for all Times end.'* "

"How encouraging," Simon said in a voice that meant far otherwise.

Above them the minute hand moved forward with a sharp snicking sound.

Alex suddenly felt the glimmer of an idea. It had something to do with what the Rabbity lady in the library had told him. He groped through his memory, trying to recall her words.

"It's changing," Miss Mumsley said suddenly.

The carved letters on the scythe were twisting, wriggling, and rearranging themselves to spell a new message.

"*'Seek not, Stranger, to pass by, / For Time doth run and Time doth fly, / And all that live are doomed to die,'*" she read.

"Another gladsome sentiment," Simon said bitterly.

The minute hand snicked again.

Then, from somewhere behind the walls, a new sound began. It was a deep rhythmic *THRUM* like the vibration of a huge bass drum. Woven through it was a high metallic whine that set Alex's teeth on edge.

"It must be that infernal machine," Miss Mumsley said.

"It sounds like it's right behind this wall," Alex said. He put a hand experimentally on the stone. "You can feel it vibrating. It's somewhere behind the clock."

The idea flickered again. He could almost reach it. It was right on the tip of his tongue. Something to do with what the Rabbity lady had said. But *what*? He racked his brain. Something about passing time by. He stared fiercely at the wooden Father Time, thinking with all his might. Father Time stared back, looking unpleasantly secretive and smug. He had a large wooden nose, tiny wooden eyes, and bushy wooden eyebrows that looked like unkempt caterpillars.

A high horrible wail rose above the thrumming of the machine, then abruptly cut off.

"What was *that*?" Simon demanded.

Tetley put his hubcap over his head.

"Doubtless some poor soul forced into the machine," Miss Mumsley said in a horrified voice.

Simon, shouting "Villains!," began pounding furiously on the wall, and Zeke, weakly, began to bark.

"We must do something!" Miss Mumsley cried. "There must be some way of getting in there! If we return to the door—"

"Time Eaters is there," Tetley protested. Hastily he put his hubcap over his head.

"We can hardly stay here," Miss Mumsley snapped.

Simon stopped pounding and began stamping his feet and clutching his hand with a pained expression.

Suddenly Alex's elusive idea turned into a startled conviction.

"No!" he said. "Not back to the door. There's another way."

"I doubt it, lad," Simon said, grimacing. His knuckles were bleeding.

"The walls is stones," Tetley said, from under the hubcap.

"Listen to what the lady in the library told me," Alex said. It made sense, he thought, in a weird sort of way. "'You must pass time by and then pass through it,' she said. Well, there's *Time,* right there. Father Time. And if you pass *by* him, there's that door that goes into the clock. Maybe there's a way to go right through it. Through the clock. *Through* time. *By* time and then *through* it. Do you see?"

"A secret passage," Simon said.

The message on the scythe had changed again. Now it read *Time can never be turned back; / It runs but forward on its track. / Seek not, O fools, to make Time stay, / For Time will sweep you all away.*

Simon curled his lip at it.

"Well, we won't know until we try," Miss Mumsley said. "And it certainly won't do us any good to just stand about here. You go ahead, Alex. It was your idea."

Alex seized the handle and tugged the glass door open.

At once the eyes of the slumbering silver moon on the clock face popped open. It glared angrily down at them. The swinging pendulum began to move faster and faster. Soon it was beating violently back and forth, slashing through the air with a vicious whipping sound.

"Careful, lad!" Simon called. "There's a weapon could break your arm."

They stared, dismayed, at the pendulum, now swinging so fast that it was a brassy blur of motion.

"There's no passing through *that*," Simon said.

Miss Mumsley tightened her lips.

"Balderdash!" she said. "There's a solution to

every problem, provided you use your head and show a little gumption."

She stepped resolutely forward and thrust her pink parasol into the path of the pendulum. There was a loud crunching sound and a snap. The parasol jerked out of Miss Mumsley's hand, sending her stumbling back against the wall. The great clock shuddered and squealed. There was a shriek of cogs grating forcibly together. The hands on the clock's face quivered and froze. Then the huge pendulum slowed, staggered, and came to a stop.

Nothing was left of Miss Mumsley's parasol but a scattering of splinters and a few tattered ribbons of pink silk. Simon brushed them aside and reached cautiously into the clock, thrusting the now-motionless pendulum out of the way.

"The lad is quite right!" he called. "There's another door here. And I wager it leads to the other side of this stony wall."

"Bravo, Alex!" Miss Mumsley said.

"Bravo yourself," Alex returned. They grinned at each other. "But I'm sorry you lost your parasol."

"A mere frippery," Miss Mumsley said, though she looked sadly, Alex thought, at the shreds of pink silk.

Simon was struggling with something inside the clock case.

"A bit cramped," he said. And then, in goaded tones, "Open, drat you!"

He twisted inside the clock, his face peering back at them, side by side with the wooden Father Time.

"The coast," he said, "would appear to be clear."

"Come along, everyone," Miss Mumsley said briskly. "Follow Simon. Come along, Tetley. You can put the hubcap down now. Come on, Zeke, brave boy. Alex, my dear."

One by one they passed through the glass door into the grandfather clock.

Behind them, in the empty stone corridor, the eyes of the silver moon slowly slid shut.

CHAPTER 23

The Time Machine

*In which Alex and his companions
are betrayed by a bird*

The room on the other side of the clock had
the look of a factory. It had high ceilings covered with odd-looking ductwork and an immac-
ulate floor covered with glassy blue tiles. A
broom and mop were propped in a corner,
and Alex had a sudden odd image of hissing
Time Eaters puttering about with dustpans and
buckets. A row of what looked like pirate treasure chests lined one wall—big round-topped

trunks with brass fittings and leather straps with buckles. There was a door at the far end of the room, above which hung a large cuckoo clock, with its little doors tightly shut. On the wall opposite the treasure chests was Urd's time machine.

The machine was an immense steel box, the size and shape of a double-decker bus. Its surface was dotted with rows of tiny blue lights that blinked rhythmically on and off, and it was making a low thrumming sound, like a monstrous metal cat purring. On its left side was a large metal funnel with a tube leading into the body of the machine. Beneath it was an ominous coffin-shaped box on a track.

"That must be where they put you," Alex said, pointing. "It rolls right inside the machine. There's a little door that slides open and a track that pulls you in."

"It makes me feel quite ill," Miss Mumsley said.

"What is *those?*" Tetley asked, pointing.

A small metal door had snapped open on the right-hand side of the machine, revealing a black-painted chute that looked a bit like a stovepipe. From the end of the chute, a series of flat silvery disks began to emerge, one after the other. They looked like big glittery cookies. The silver disks moved steadily forward, propelled by a whirring conveyor belt. When they reached the end of the belt, they toppled with little crunchy thuds into a large metal barrel.

Alex, Simon, and Miss Mumsley exchanged puzzled looks.

"Cakes?" Simon said incredulously.

"How peculiar," Miss Mumsley said.

Simon strode over to the barrel, leaned over, and seized one of the cookies.

"There are letters upon it," he said. He held the cookie close to his nose.

"'One Lifetime,'" he read.

"Of course," Miss Mumsley said. "Each of those cakes represents a life's worth of time." Her voice quavered slightly. "Stolen from some helpless prisoner."

"Pure time," Simon said musingly. "So this is what yon unpleasant lady nibbles to keep herself as young as a half-grown girl."

Alex looked wildly from the time machine—still steadily generating cookies—to Zeke and back again.

"So that stuff makes you younger?" he said excitedly. "So if Zeke ate a piece"—his words fell over each other in eagerness—"he'd get younger. He'd have his time back again!"

"But how much to feed him?" Miss Mumsley murmured. "I've heard that one year in a dog's life is the same as seven years to a human being. So if one of these cakes is a human lifetime . . ."

"So a seventh part of a cake is a dog lifetime," Simon said pompously, raising a finger in the air. "So a bit less than a seventh part . . ."

"These cakes cannot be divided into seven parts," he said angrily, a few minutes later. The floor at his feet was littered was broken cookies.

"Never mind, Simon dear," Miss Mumsley said.

Alex sighed. "I'll just give him a sliver," he said, "and see what happens."

Zeke was lying, exhausted, on the floor, his gray head pillowed on his paws. Alex knelt beside him, gently petting his ears. Zeke woofed weakly and tried to wag his tail.

"Here, boy," Alex said. He held out a silver cookie fragment. "Eat this."

For a dreadful moment, he thought he was too late. Zeke gave a long rattling sigh and closed his eyes.

"Zeke?" Alex said.

The old dog lay there, gray and worn and utterly still. When Alex touched him, his fur felt harsh and cold.

"Alex," Miss Mumsley said gently. It was the sort of voice, Alex knew, that grownups used to tell you something perfectly awful. His eyes burned with tears.

"Zeke!" he cried frantically. "Just try, boy, try! Just this one time. Please. *Please.*"

He held the cookie sliver to Zeke's lips.

Then, very slowly, Zeke's ribs heaved again and he put out his tongue and took the cookie into his mouth.

For a long minute nothing happened. Alex held his breath. Then something began to change. At first it was just a darkening of the gray fur. It reminded Alex of the way the trees unfolded their leaves in springtime on the hills beyond the town, the green first appearing on the trees closest to the bottom, then creeping slowly up the hill toward the summit, changing slowly as it traveled from yellow-green to lime green to deep dark emerald and olive. On Zeke's ears and muzzle and back, the gray rippled and shifted, changing from tan to toast to golden brown. Then his paws paddled, as if he were having a dream about racing rabbits, and his ears wavered and stood up. He opened his eyes and scrambled to his feet, wriggling out from beneath Alex's hand.

"It's working!" Miss Mumsley cried.

Alex found he couldn't speak. He felt as if his heart were about to burst.

Zeke gave a joyous bark and began to leap from one to another of the clustered company, wagging his tail ecstatically. He sprang upon Simon, causing him to stagger backward, butted his head adoringly against Miss Mumsley's pink skirt, licked Alex's face from forehead to chin, and flung himself gleefully upon Tetley, who promptly fell over backward, dropping his hub-cap with a clang. Then he began to run madly up and down the room, as if his newly returned energy were just too much to keep inside.

"The portion was just right," Simon said with satisfaction.

"So that problem is dealt with," Miss Mumsley said briskly, in the manner of someone efficiently checking things off a list. "And now I suggest we proceed to the next. One, we must find Alex's watch so that he will be able to return to his home. And two, as responsible citizens, we must somehow do away with that wretched machine."

Alex pulled his eyes away from the galloping Zeke to stare hopelessly at the huge thrumming machine. It looked immovable and solid, a smooth impenetrable mass of metal. Their chance of destroying it, Alex reflected, was about as likely as their chance of knocking over the Great Wall of China.

"Do away with it?" he repeated. "But *how*?"

"We hits it?" Tetley suggested hopefully. He brandished his hubcap.

"We don't want to merely damage it, Tetley," Miss Mumsley said. "We want to utterly eradicate it. We need to think of something more effective." She tightened her lips. "Something lethal."

"If we but had some gunpowder," Simon said longingly. "Or a catapult."

"Or something dreadful to pour into that funnel," Miss Mumsley said. "Tar, perhaps."

"Bubblegums," Tetley said.

"Glue."

"Molasses."

"Well, we don't have any molasses," Miss Mumsley said. "We must think of something else."

They prowled about the machine, prodding at it and looking vainly for weak spots. Urd and her Time Eaters had done a dismayingly good job. There were no cracks or crevices or loose pieces, nothing to pull off or pry apart or shatter. The surface of the machine was as smooth as a bowling ball. They could see themselves reflected in it.

"What makes it go?" Alex asked suddenly.

"There aren't any controls or anything. Just those little lights."

"Curious," Simon said. "Perhaps in the back?"

But the back of the machine was as blank and featureless as the front.

"On top?" Alex said, craning his neck to peer upward.

Zeke gave an excited yip.

"I bet I could climb up there."

"I'll take that wager, lad," Simon said, "and give you a good leg up."

The climb, Alex soon found, was easier said than done. Climbing the machine was like scaling a sheer wall of ice. Simon's boost landed him on the track with the wheeled coffin—Alex saw, with a shiver, that it was equipped inside with leather straps and manacles. From there, he hoisted himself unsteadily up the side of the funnel, clinging like a monkey to its slippery sides and scrabbling with his sneakers. For every foot that he managed to haul himself up, it seemed that he slid half that length back down again. It was a slow, miserable, frustrating business, made slower by his increasingly desperate feeling that time—his time on the Blue Moon—was rapidly running out.

The stretch above the funnel was even worse, since there was nothing to cling to at all except a little lip of metal that ran around the very top of the machine. At last, with an enormous kick and heave, Alex flung himself stomach-first over the edge. He wriggled into a sitting position and sat there for a moment, panting, his head just brushing the ceiling. Then he looked around.

"I think this is it," he said.

The top of the machine was set with rows of knobs and dials. There were labels reading *Hours, Days, Weeks,* and *Years* and some complicated-looking gauges marked mysteriously in "Mhz" and "Psi." There were some colored cranks—they looked rather like the handles that turned on the water to the garden hose in Alex's backyard at home—and a big metal lever that could be set to either ON or OFF. At the moment, it was ON. Alex took a deep breath, seized the lever in both hands, and moved it to OFF.

There was an instant of absolute silence. They had grown so accustomed to the pounding thrum of the machine that the sudden cessation of sound was startling. Zeke and Tetley pawed confusedly at their ears.

Then the little wooden doors of the cuckoo clock sprang open and the cuckoo popped out. It was the wickedest-looking bird Alex had ever seen, a little metal monster with sharp steel feathers, a long pointed beak, and a pair of glittery little eyes made of diamond chips. It flapped its metal wings twice, opened its beak, and began to scream at the top of its voice.

"Trespassers!" it shrieked. *"Trespassers! Trespassers! Trespassers!"*

CHAPTER 24

Time Turned Back

In which Alex is a hero

*T*respassers! Trespassers! Thieves and spies!"

Simon dived for the cuckoo clock.

"Silence that thing!" Miss Mumsley shouted, while Zeke barked ferociously and Simon bellowed terrible threats about tearing screechy little heads off and baking tin-pot birds alive in pies.

But they were too late. The bird had already sounded the alarm.

A door at the far end of the room was flung open, and there stood Urd. Now she was wearing a pale-green dress belted with shimmery rainbow-colored ribbons. There were green slippers on her slim feet and a silver circlet bound around her curly golden hair. She looked furious. Behind her, tall and shadowed, loomed the clustered figures of the Time Eaters.

"You!" Urd spat. "How dare you!"

She wasn't pretty now at all, Alex thought, with her face twisted in rage and her eyes cold and narrow. In fact, she looked a lot like the nasty cuckoo-clock bird.

"How *dare* you touch my machine! How *dare* you think to stand in my way! You, with your puny pinches of time!"

She twirled on a pale-green toe like a ballerina, pointing at each of them in turn.

"But nothing can stop me! You're right where I want you, and now you can watch as one by one, I take your time away!"

She pointed a slender finger at Zeke, who growled.

"Snarl away, my furry friend, for when I've done, there'll be nothing left of *you* but skin and bones."

She whirled again, laughing, to point at Miss Mumsley.

"And *you,* my sharp-spoken lady, how will you like it when *he*"—she twirled to point at Simon—"is drained of all his time, withered as a mummy in a box?"

She turned on Tetley, who hugged his hubcap tightly but stood his ground.

"I'm not afraid of you and they," Tetley said stoutly, but in a quavery voice.

"You will be," Urd said darkly. "When your turn comes."

The Time Eaters leaned and hissed together, sounding like Halloween wind in a field of old dried corn.

"Where is the boy?" Urd cried suddenly. She twirled again, making her ribbons ripple and her green skirts flare. "Where is the boy?"

Alex crouched, frozen, on top of the machine.

"I do not know, madam," Simon said coldly.

"He left," Miss Mumsley said, staring determinedly at a point just above Urd's left shoulder.

Zeke gave a yipping bark that sounded like a snicker.

"He is gone away," Tetley said.

"Danger! Danger! Danger!"

It was the cuckoo bird. It rocketed out of its clock and sped around the room, then paused, hovering in the air above the machine, glaring straight at Alex with venomous little eyes.

"Trespassers! Trespassers! Trespassers! Spies! Spies! Spies!"

Urd looked up and her lovely face went ugly again.

"Come down at once!" she cried.

"No!" Simon and Miss Mumsley shouted at the same time.

Urd signaled with a hand, and two of the Time Eaters moved toward Simon. They paced across the tiled floor like dark smoke, wafting before them a cold smell of decay.

"Come down, boy," Urd cried gleefully. "Come down—or stay and watch them feed."

She had put on her crystal spectacles, which sparkled with rainbow lights whenever she turned her head.

"Come down!" she shrieked. Her voice sounded like fingernails scraping on a blackboard. "Come down and I will spare your friends!"

"No!" Simon shouted again.

"Look around you, Alex!" Miss Mumsley cried. "There's something up there that she doesn't want you to find!"

Alex looked frantically around. There were the knobs and dials and cranks, and the big metal lever—but he'd already turned that OFF. There was nothing else. Not a single thing.

He watched helplessly as, below him, the Time Eaters slowly advanced and his friends, huddled together, slowly moved backward. Simon had put his arm around Miss Mumsley. Zeke was growling furiously. Miss Mumsley was holding Tetley's paw.

Backward!

The idea exploded in Alex's brain like one of the Moon Rats' fireworks. What had Father Time's message said, back there on the great grandfather clock? *Time can never be turned back; / It runs but forward on its track.*

So what would happen, Alex thought, if I made the machine run *backward*? Would it just fall apart? Is that what Urd is frightened of? Cautiously he set his hand on the big metal lever. As he did, the cuckoo screamed. It sped toward him down the length of the room, screeching as it came. The sharp feathers of its wings fanned the air like knives. It plummeted toward Alex, diamond eyes blazing, jabbing and stabbing with its vicious beak.

Alex beat wildly at his attacker, but the bird kept on coming. Its wings made a noise like the spinning blades of a blender. Screaming, it dived at Alex's face.

On the floor below, Zeke was howling and leaping at the side of the machine. Miss Mumsley and Simon were shouting angrily. Simon was threatening to melt the bird into porridge or hammer it into roasting spits. Tetley was jumping up and down, and vigorously but ineffectively throwing bent nails.

Alex ducked away from the bird, wrapping an arm around his head. He lunged forward and, with his free hand, seized the great metal lever and thrust it violently backward as far as it would go. There was a hideous squealing and grinding of gears. Then, from somewhere deep within the machine, something began to thrum. It sounded like someone beating on a big bass drum. The thrumming sound grew louder and faster. The metal bird gave one last earsplitting screech, fled back to its clock, and disappeared inside.

Urd was gesturing violently and screaming something at the Time Eaters, but Alex couldn't hear her above the vibrating thrum of the machine. Her little pink mouth was open wide, and her crystal spectacles burned like fire.

The machine was running backward. From his high perch, Alex saw the silver cookies sucked back out of their barrel and into the machine's belly. Beneath him, the metal framework heaved and bucked. There was a screech of tearing metal and Alex saw that the hands on the dials were spinning like tops. The glass face of one dial shattered, and then another. The machine seemed to be shaking itself to pieces. It shuddered and shrieked and spat out a stream of black and silver dust. There was a sound of crashing and falling and a long expiring whine. All the blue lights went out.

The dust hovered hesitantly in the air. Then it thickened, moved purposefully toward Urd and the Time Eaters, and fell upon them. It vanished before it reached the ground.

Urd was dancing in fury, her little green shoes pounding up and down on the glassy tiles.

"Seize them!" she gasped.

The Time Eaters, moving as one, stepped forward and raised their staffs. Beneath the dark hoods, there was a flash of phosphorescent eyes, and from their unseen mouths came a long whispery hiss.

Simon clenched his fists and stepped forward, but Miss Mumsley put a restraining hand on his arm.

"Something's happening," she said.

Something was wrong with the Time Eaters.

"Seize them!" Urd shrieked. There was a note of fear in her voice. The crystal spectacles blazed even brighter.

But the Time Eaters were no longer able to

do her bidding. All together, their staffs thudded on the floor—and fell clattering to the tiles, dropped from suddenly lifeless hands. The Time Eaters slowly collapsed like pricked balloons. For a moment, their withered blue hands clawed the air and a moan spread through their ranks, a sound like winter wind in dead trees. Then they shriveled into nothingness. Alex stared, astonished, at what was left behind: a clutter of fallen staffs, rows of empty cloaks. The Time Eaters were utterly gone.

"Can you get down, Alex?" Miss Mumsley asked into the stunned silence.

"I think so," Alex said. He began to slide carefully down the side of the now blank and motionless machine, clutching for hand- and footholds. As he reached the floor, he realized that now something was also happening to Urd.

She had dropped her crystal spectacles, and her eyes, uncovered, were round with horror.

"No!" she said in a pleading voice. She took two hasty steps backward, twisting her hands in the folds of her gauzy green skirt. "Oh, no!"

"What's happening?" Alex asked.

"It's time," Simon replied from behind him, in a hushed voice. "I think it's time caught up with her at last, as it did with them." He pointed at the cloaks of the vanished Time Eaters. "When you ran that devilish machine backward, it spewed out the opposite of time. Time in reverse. It cancels out true time—time forward. It brings things back in balance. Urd, she'd taken more than her fair share of time, and now that's gone. She's going back to where she began."

"I don't understand," Alex said.

"It's mathematics, lad," Simon said. "You add some, then subtract the same amount, and you're right back whence you started."

Urd buried her face in her hands. When she lifted it again, everything was changed. The golden curls were gone, along with the pink cheeks, the ribbons, and the dancing shoes. An old, old woman stood there, bent, wrinkled, and gray.

"By Saint Winifred's wig stand," Simon said in an awed voice under his breath.

Urd pointed a bony finger at Alex and gave a cry of rage.

CHAPTER 25

Lost Time

*In which a goddess takes
a hand*

They stood looking at the ancient crone who, just moments ago, had been a slip of a golden girl. Urd glared at them with rheumy eyes, her twisted finger pointing at Alex, trembling with rage.

"*You!*" she rasped. "This is your fault! Yours! And I'll see that you pay for it, my sweet lad. Your task is not over yet—nor will ever be, my dearie; I'll see to that. You'll live to be sorry indeed that ever you crossed paths with me!"

She hobbled swiftly across the floor to the chests that stood along the wall opposite the broken machine and began to unbuckle the straps and fling back the lids.

"Here's your lost time, my pet, though little good it will do you!"

The chests were filled to the brim with timepieces. There were wristwatches and pocket watches and watches on chains, meant to be worn as pendants around the neck. There were a lot of alarm clocks, most of which seemed to be broken, as if some sleeper had flung them impatiently to the floor. There was a child's clock in the shape of a teddy bear—the hands had been torn off it—and an old-fashioned wooden clock in a case painted with pansies and a glow-in-the-dark purple neon clock shaped like a doughnut. The purple parts kept flickering off and on and making a crackling noise.

"They're all here," Urd cackled spitefully.

"Hourglasses that have lost their sand, musical clocks that have lost their chimes, water clocks run dry, and sundials left in shadow. There are clocks wound too tight and clocks wound too little, calendar clocks that failed to leap over leap year, seven-day clocks that stopped at six days, and stopwatches that never stopped at all. There are schoolroom clocks that sent the children home too early, and factory clocks that sent the workers home too late, and a hospital clock whose ticking sounded like a deathwatch beetle, so they tossed it in the rubbish bin."

She stooped to rummage in a brimming chest, cackling all the time.

"Lost seconds, lost minutes, lost hours and days and weeks, lost months—why, the entire Julian calendar is here, that lost ten days all at once in 1582 and hasn't been heard of since."

She straightened up creakily, clutching her back.

"My watch!" Alex cried, jumping forward with his hands outstretched.

It was crammed in the top left-hand corner of the second chest. It was his missing pocket watch. He would have known it anywhere. There on the cover was the engraving of the strange little two-faced man, looking at the same time to the right and to the left. There it was. He suddenly felt as light as air. He'd found the watch, and the Moon was still blue. His troubles were over. He could get back home after all.

"Janus," Simon murmured. "The two-faced god. Looking both forward and back."

"What an exquisite timepiece," Miss Mumsley said.

Urd looked furious.

"Not so fast, my lovely boy," she said. And before Alex had time to move, she darted forward and snatched the dangling watch out of his grasp. She held it just beyond his reach, cackling with glee.

"Now you may want, but want must be your master, for you'll not have your trinket back from me. Now let *you* be the one to suffer and moan, trapped here as you'll be"—her voice rose to a shriek— *"forever and ever!"*

"That watch," Miss Mumsley said sharply,

"rightfully belongs to Alex. He found it. You must return it to him at once. Anything else would be the basest theft."

"Aye, and what did he do to *me*?" the Norn snapped back. "Killed my servants and stole my time, *stole my ti-i-ime*."

For a moment, her voice wavered upward into a keening wail.

"This is my revenge, my downy chick. Here may you sit for all eternity, and I wish you the joy of it!"

"If we all rushed at her together," Simon muttered hurriedly, "approaching from several directions and shouting in a distracting manner . . ."

"She disappears," Tetley said. "You can't catch they. They disappears. They goes out—*bink!*—like a bulb light."

"Please!" Alex said desperately. "Please give it back!"

Urd was giggling, in a high tinkly voice that sounded like the young girl she had been before. Alex hadn't liked her then either.

"She's going, she is," said Tetley.

The Norn, still giggling, was growing transparent around the edges, slowly fading out of focus.

She's taking her time about it, Alex thought despairingly. *Dragging it out on purpose.* He felt sick.

Then, suddenly, there was a tremendous flash of brilliant silver light.

"That," a cross voice said, "is quite enough!"

It was a goddess.

She was dressed in a long glimmering robe the color of clouds and stars, and on her head was a slender silver crown made of blue diamonds and milk-white moonstones. Her silvery hair streamed down her back, and her face was serene and remote, a face of cold and awesome power. The face of a queen.

Behind her stood another goddess, in a robe the shifting color of mist and moondust. She wore a crown of opals and pearls, and her hair flared out in a halo around her head, as silver-white as moonlit frost. It took Alex a moment to recognize the Rabbity lady from the library in this new guise. *So that must be her sister, Selena,* he thought, trying not to stare. *The one who gets so huffy if people are late.*

Tetley and Simon were bowing low, and even Miss Mumsley dropped a restrained curtsy. Alex found himself bowing too.

"I do not interfere with the Norns," Selena said. "They keep to themselves, going about their business, and I keep to mine."

She paused, looking sternly at Urd.

"But there are limits."

Urd opened her mouth in protest, but no sound came out.

There was a shimmer in the air and, on either side of Urd, appeared Verdande, with her spindle and her basket of wool, and Skuld, with her silver scissors.

"You see, fool girl, what comes of meddling with time," Verdande said.

"Too big for your britches," Skuld said, clacking her scissors open and shut.

Urd looked sullen.

"It seems to me," the moon goddess said coldly, "that this problem should have been dealt with long before. Look at the damage that has been done, while you sat by and did nothing."

"I spin," Verdande said.

"I snip," said Skuld.

"All eventually resolves itself," they said together.

"But it has not!" Selena said in a voice like thunder.

Tetley dropped to the floor and put his hubcap over his head.

"And now," the moon goddess said, "Urd has interfered with this child's search and has stolen what he has found."

The Norns bent toward each other, muttering, bringing their heads close together.

"What is, is," Verdande said. "And what will be, will be. It is not for us to meddle."

"But the boy has done us a service," Skuld said, clacking her scissors.

"And even the Norns repay their debts," Verdande said.

"Here, boy." Skuld held out the pocket watch. The little silver head twisted dizzily back and forth, dangling from its chain. "Take your timepiece. And be more careful with it in the future."

She turned to Urd.

"And for you, my lass, there's a roomful of wool to sort and scrub. I hope you've learned a lesson."

Skuld and Verdande each seized one of Urd's arms, holding her firmly above the elbows. They nodded shortly in Selena's direction, and the goddess nodded majestically back. Then they disappeared.

"So you did it after all!" Lulu said brightly. "Lost heart, lost way, and lost time, all accounted for, and a tidy job you all made of it, if I do say so myself. Why, we never thought you'd manage, did we, Selena, what with the tollgate and the maze around the tower and all those dreadful Time Eaters and the Norns—not much help *they* are, when all's said and done—but you did it, and destroyed that wretched time machine to boot. Why, I think you're heroes, each and every one of you, and if my sister doesn't see fit to tell you so, I do!"

"Now, Lulu," Selena said repressively.

She raised both hands high in the air, and a light began to pulse around her, growing brighter and brighter by the moment until Alex could no longer bear to look at it. They seemed to be floating upward. There was a rushing sound in his ears. The walls of Urd's castle melted, fell away, and vanished. Then everything went dark.

CHAPTER 26

Some Endings and a Beginning

*In which Simon takes on
a difficult task*

Alex gaped in surprise.

Suddenly they were in an old-fashioned Victorian parlor. There were flowered carpets, a nubbly wallpaper with a pattern of drunken-looking peacocks, and a lot of little footstools upholstered in needlepoint. A fire burned brightly in a marble fireplace, and a table in the center of the floor was set for tea. At the far end of the table, half hidden behind a bulbous silver teapot, sat Lulu. She peeked brightly at Alex over the spout of the pot and gave him a cheerful little wave.

"Sit down, do, all of you," she said, "and make yourselves right at home. And this *is* Selena, dear, my sister, the one I was telling you about. Do you take lemon or sugar? And would you like a crumpet? Or a slice of seedy cake? We don't have very long to chat, of course, because the Blue is almost over and now that you've found what you came for, you'll be wanting to get home again. All's well that ends well; that's what Selena always says, and I'm sure she's right. She usually is."

"How you do run on, Lulu," Selena said.

She was sitting in a high-backed armchair next to the fire, and there was a silver shimmer around her. When she rose to her feet, the rest of the company hastily rose too, except for Lulu, who was placidly buttering crumpets.

The goddess ran her cool steel-gray eyes over the assembly and paused on Tetley, who cringed and tentatively raised his hubcap.

"It wasn't me," he said in a guilty voice.

Selena smiled and shook her head.

"You have done very well, Tetley," she said. "You have been a brave and resourceful companion and a loyal friend."

She bent down and placed her finger on Tetley's hubcap. There was a shower of blue sparks, and when she drew away her hand, the hubcap had become a smooth circle of silver, ornamented in the center with a gleaming golden crescent moon.

"In recognition of your courage and kindness, I bestow upon you the title of First Rat, with all the perquisites of the position, reporting directly to the Goddesses of the Moon."

Tetley—his whiskers trembling violently— pulled himself proudly erect.

Alex could hear him ecstatically repeating "First Rat" and "perquisites" under his breath.

"And as for the rest of you," the goddess went on, "you have done us a great service, and we are deeply in your debt. Alexander Bailey, Edith Mumsley, Simon Nash, and Zeke the dog—your names will be remembered with honor in the House of Records and indeed throughout the country of the Moon. I am glad to see that your tasks are completed, that what was lost is safely found, and that we can reward you by returning you now to your own times and places. My sister and I wish you well."

"Please wait a moment," Miss Mumsley said.

She and Simon came forward to stand, arm in arm, before the moon goddess.

"We would like, Mr. Nash and I—" she began hesitantly.

Simon interrupted. "Miss Mumsley has greatly honored me by consenting to become my wife," he said. "We wish to be returned together."

Alex looked from one to the other in delighted astonishment.

"But I thought . . ." he stammered. Hadn't Simon criticized the feminine mind? And hadn't Miss Mumsley said that she could take care of herself?

"I had never thought to meet a lady of such courage and forthright mind," Simon said.

"Or I a gentleman so dependable and kind," said Miss Mumsley softly.

There was a babble of congratulations,

hurriedly silenced when Selena again raised her hand.

"I am sorry," she said, "but it is impossible."

Simon and Miss Mumsley exchanged horrified looks.

"Oh, no," Miss Mumsley said in a choked voice.

Alex could hardly stand to look at their stricken faces.

"Why?" he demanded.

"It's really quite simple, dear," Lulu answered, "but *most* unfair if you ask me, since the point, once you've gone to all this trouble, is a happy ending; otherwise no one would bother to try at all, would they, and then where would we be? But it's all quite, quite clear. Once you've found your lost item, you must be immediately transported back to your own place and time. Not to someone else's place and time or a place and time that you choose for yourself, on a whim. No, back to where you came from—that's the way it works, and there's no getting around it. It's a temporal translocation problem. That's what the Blue is, you know. I thought I explained."

"It has to do with the nature of time," Selena said. "Mr. Nash and Miss Mumsley have their own places in time and these cannot be changed."

"But there must be *some* way," Alex said. What had Miss Mumsley said? "There's a solution to every problem, provided you use your head and show a little gumption."

Lulu waved a crumpet, scattering crumbs. "Why, that's exactly what you say yourself, Selena. Time and again, I've heard you. 'Show a little gumption, Lulu, do,' you say, and now they *have,* so I think it's up to us to try and think of something, seeing how much they've done."

Selena was silent for a moment, staring into the fire.

"There is one way," she said finally. "But there are certain difficulties."

Simon and Miss Mumsley looked at each other with dawning hope.

"I will do anything," Simon said, at the same time that Miss Mumsley said, "What difficulties?"

"Time passes differently on the Moon," Selena said. "In fact, it passes not at all, as you mortals know it. Which is why our worlds meet only during the rare periods when temporal translocation is possible. That is, when the Moon is blue. For Mr. Nash to reach Miss Mumsley's time, he would be forced to wait here, counting out—how many years lie between you?"

Simon counted rapidly on his fingers.

"Three hundred and eighteen," he said. "And two months."

"To pass through three hundred and eighteen years, you would have to—time them. You would have to remain here on the Moon until you have counted them out, hour by hour, day by day. It is a dreadfully long and lonely task, and those who attempt it often fail."

"But not *all,* Selena!" Lulu cried. "Not all! Why, I remember—"

"You'll need my watch," Alex said. He felt a pang as he said it, but he knew suddenly that it was true. "You'll need a way of keeping track."

He pulled it slowly out of his pocket and

took one last look at the two-faced little bearded man before placing it firmly in Simon's hand.

Three hundred and eighteen years, he thought. *That's a horribly long time.*

Selena nodded approvingly.

"One hundred and sixteen thousand and seventy days," she said briskly. "Two million, seven hundred and eighty-five thousand, six hundred and eighty hours."

"I can do it," Simon said firmly.

Miss Mumsley's eyes filled with tears.

"I will be waiting, Simon dear," she said.

Alex later remembered the departure from the Moon as a confusing blur. He and Zeke were hugged all around—by Tetley, by Simon and Miss Mumsley, and even by Lulu, who forgot herself in the excitement of the moment. There were thanks to all, from all, and promises never to forget, and Tetley produced a much-written-upon scrap of paper and asked for everyone's autograph.

Then Selena had them line up before the door next to a faded aspidistra plant. She raised her hand and pointed a silvery finger at Miss Mumsley. Miss Mumsley for an instant was outlined in blue light. Alex's last glimpse showed her standing resolutely straight, shoulders back, her hat with the painted cherries planted firmly on the top of her head. Then she was gone.

Then it was Alex's turn. He reached down and gripped Zeke's collar. The goddess raised her hand, and there was a sound of rushing wind in his ears.

As he vanished from the Moon, Alex seemed to see the whole strange country laid out beneath him, now swept clear of its enveloping blue mist. There were the stone spires and stained-glass windows of the House of Records, the cottage by the tollgate, the Gallery of Ar, and the blinking neon lights of the Moondust Café. There was the Inn of Abandoned Plans—it looked more ramshackle than ever—and the glittering Crystal Forest, and the Pointless Tower, with its endlessly spinning arrow. Far in the distance was the castle where Urd had lived with her Time Eaters. It looked dark and lonely on its soaring cliff, and Alex wondered if anyone would ever live in it again.

Then, for an instant, he seemed to see a stream of people, bidding him farewell. There were the Moon Rats, shrieking and jumping up and down—he could see Perline wildly waving her pink bicycle helmet—and the crow lady, scolding about willful waste. He saw Sebastian waving his lute, Reggie and his mates, cheering and waving their map, Jonathan Periwinkle, waving a tattered list, and the Hare, elegant in blue brocade, waving his mallet. Then there was Tetley, sniffling and waving his hubcap, and finally, at the very last, there was Simon, with the watch on a table in front of him, smiling and raising a hand.

He'd learned so much on his journey, Alex reflected, but already it was becoming dreamlike and hard to remember. *Discover your talents,* someone had said, and *Follow through on your good intentions,* and *Time isn't wasted if you're doing what you love best.* There was Simon, looking solemn, explaining how learning made time worthwhile. It was all beginning to jumble together somehow and to seem very far away.

The last thing he remembered was the cool voice of Selena, the Moon Goddess, speaking in his ear: *You have done well, Alexander, and all will be well.*

CHAPTER 27

On and On and On

*In which Alex receives a message
from some old friends*

In one sense, it was as if Alex had never been away. In another, it was if he had been away for a long, long time. Nothing was different, but at the same time everything had changed.

A lot of trash had been pilfered from the backyard—"Which saves me a trip to the landfill," Alex's father said. "Though why anyone would want all that junk . . ."—and Alex's awful report card and its accompanying letter had simply vanished, as if they had never existed. Alex decided not to ask about them.

The frightening sense of time rushing by him and vanishing into nothingness was gone now. His troubles at school seemed to have evaporated too. He no longer felt as if time were speeding past him, leaving him behind. Instead time seemed to stretch out before him, rich and exciting, filled with new things to do. He was choosing how to use it. *Choose time or lose time*—he thought perhaps he knew what that meant now. Sometimes he could almost feel Simon, peering over his shoulder, eagerly learning with him, discovering a bigger world.

Zeke seemed unaffected by his strange journey and his awful encounter with the Time Eaters, but Alex sometimes saw him with his paws on the windowsill at night, gazing up at the Moon. Alex suspected that he missed Simon and Miss Mumsley and Tetley. He knew just how Zeke felt. He missed them too.

Some weeks after his return, Alex received a package. It arrived in an official-looking envelope, delivered by special courier. The return address was a legal firm in Ohio. Alex had to sign for it. Inside was a carefully wrapped packet tied with a red cord and a typed letter.

Dear Sir, the letter read.

In accordance with the terms of the will of Alexander Mumsley Nash, my late client, I enclose the accompanying bequest. I was instructed to tell you that it was greatly treasured by my client's ancestor, Simon Nash, who never permitted it to leave his side.

Sincerely,
Robert P. Rowell, Esq.
Rowell, Buxtable, & Steel
Attorneys at Law

The packet contained Alex's watch, carefully polished and wrapped in layers of cotton wool. With it was an old-fashioned sepia-tinted photograph in a dark wood frame. The photograph, Alex realized with a shock, was of Simon and Miss Mumsley.

Miss Mumsley, in a long flowered dress with puffy sleeves, was sitting in a straight chair, while Simon, looking peculiar in a frock coat with silver buttons, stood beside her with a hand on her shoulder. They were both smiling. On her lap, Miss Mumsley held a small girl wearing an enormous hair bow, and at Simon's side stood a little boy wearing short pants and a jacket with a round collar. Prominently propped beside Miss Mumsley's chair was a large and very frilly parasol. Though everything in the photograph was a faded brownish color, Alex just knew that that parasol was rose pink.

Tucked into the frame was a slip of paper with another note. This one was written by hand. Reading it, Alex felt his eyes prick with tears.

"For Alex, with our deepest devotion and everlasting gratitude," the note said, in a flowing copperplate that Alex knew must be Miss Mumsley's—Mrs. Nash's, he hastily corrected

himself. And below that, in a spiky script that he knew must be Simon's, was written: *"May the Norns spin for you a long and golden thread, Alexander, as they have for Edith and me—and always remember that though time passes, friendship is eternal, and love and joy and wonder go ever on and on and on. . . ."*

Acknowledgments

Many thanks to all the people who made this book possible, among them Joshua Rupp for his thoughtful and creative suggestions, Caleb Rupp for his imaginative input, Ethan Rupp for his artistic vision and unfailing ability to deal with computer malfunctions, and Pauline Fadden for her constant support and kind heart. I am eternally grateful to Cynthia Platt, my wonderful editor, whose perceptive questions and comments made *Journey to the Blue Moon* the book it ultimately became; and to all the talented and dedicated book lovers at Candlewick Press. And, of course, many thanks always to my husband, Randy, for whom I would count out any amount of time on the Blue Moon.